WESKER ON THEATRE

Arnold Wesker

Wesker On Theatre

A selection of essays, lectures and journalism

OBERON BOOKS

LONDON

First published in 2010 by Oberon Books Ltd
521 Caledonian Road, London N7 9RH
Tel: 020 7607 3637 / Fax: 020 7607 3629
e-mail: info@oberonbooks.com
www.oberonbooks.com

ISBN: 978-1-84002-986-4

Printed in Great Britain by CPI Antony Rowe, Chippenham

Preface

Writers can be divided into those intrigued by what they have written and those who believe art to be a mysterious process, inexplicable, beyond the control of the writer. There is a third group, mainly academics, who believe the creative process *is* explicable but that creators are not the people best suited or equipped to know what they have done; only the informed scholar, uninvolved in the process – and therefore objective – can best analyse and explain.

I once thought I belonged to the first group: that I understood what I was doing in terms of structure, rhythm and meaning. Then I found myself unable to explain how the first lines of some of the plays arrived. I also came to recognise that there were two perspectives to a play: looking forward to the play one had set out to write, and looking back at the play one had written, not always the same thing. The process was perhaps more mysterious than I'd imagined possible.

I did not subscribe quite so tolerantly to the third group – the objective scholar – since I doubted the existence of that regal state, objectivity. How objective could one be, especially a scholar weighed down with so many other opinions from here there and everywhere. The best one could expect from the scholar – and blessed with a fine mind it is a pretty good 'best' – is to be informed of a huge basket of the world's dramatic output alongside which to make comparisons. The scholar could compare; objectivity was a more dubious quality.

More to the point (despite appearing to contradict myself) every time a writer crossed out a word, a line, a paragraph they were being objective about the words they had rejected.

As for the quality of being 'uninvolved' – I was not sure I saw the virtue in that since it led to many elements in the play being missed. The 'involved' writer knew what had been missed, and despaired of ever being fully understood or recognised for what had been put into the work. Nevertheless I understood the importance of distance from the work which is why I left draft after draft alone for long periods before going back to produce another draft.

All these shifts of thought were, over the years, put into essays and lectures some of which I've assembled in this volume. Some have been published elsewhere but this is the first time an assortment of theatre pieces have been brought together exploring such subjects as *The DNA of a Play; Interpretation – to explain or impose; The*

Nature of Theatre Dialogue; Can playwrights be taught to write plays? and many others that attempt to explain what I think I've been doing during fifty years of a theatre writing career. Many will find my observations controversial. I would like to think they are thought-provoking.

February 2010, Hove

Contents

1. To Cheat, to Pretend

Perhaps the first thing that should be observed of the theatre is that it is endowed with an enormous power to cheat. To cheat is not the same as to pretend.

Actors are called upon to 'pretend' – to be who they are not. The set-designer is called upon to pretend that one stage-flat is an entire room. The writer is called upon to pretend that two hours can represent a character's-life time, or that light-changes are the passing of days. The director is the only one who is not called upon to pretend. His/hers is another function: to prevent the actor, designer, and writer from cheating.

All three can call upon resources, that will enable them to cheat. Cheating is using the powerfully emotive elements of sound, lighting, voice, music, colour, and shape to persuade an audience that something significant or substantial is taking place on stage when in fact it isn't. Paradoxically, although the director's function is to prevent his team cheating – rather like the police inspector's job is to prevent crime, yet the director is in *the* key position to cheat more than the others, just as the police inspector, because of his authority, is in a key position to commit crime without detection.

To be specific: the director can encourage the set designer to create a vast impressive set which can communicate an importance about the events unfolding even though those events are anecdotal, without importance; he can call from the lighting designer a sequence of lights which create an atmosphere the text doesn't really substantiate; he can direct the actor to pause, look, and dramatically poise his body to make it seem that something profound is taking place when in fact nothing has happened or been said that earns that moment of apparent profundity. And of course the director can use that most potent of all the art forms, music, to help make it seem that something ominous or tragic is taking place when in fact nothing is.

To do all these things is to cheat.

To have lived with a child on stage for many scenes and then for it to die has earned the actress playing the mother the right to mourn in silence at the bedside. Then the pauses and the body poised in anguish are actions belonging to substance. The pause and the anguish may be pretend-pauses and pretend-anguish, but they are honourable pretences, acceptable within the profession of acting for having been *earned.*

To cheat, to pretend; earned or unearned. It's important to distinguish between the two.

Stockholm, 6 November 1996

2. The DNA of a play – lasting through time and crossing frontiers

THE QUESTION IS often asked: what makes a play last through time and able to cross frontiers? To answer this question we need to break down the structure of a dramatic work into its DNA. If we can identify the DNA structure of a play we might then be able to identify which part of the structure makes it last through time. To do this I would like briefly to look at my own work, which, it is supposed, I know most about.

The first observation to be made is that we are not talking about categories. All writers hope that the texture of their work is too rich and varied to be reduced to the simple categories frequently applied by journalists who are too rushed to reflect at any serious level, and by some academics who should know better. If you've heard of me at all it will probably be under the nonsense category of 'social realist' – a term which means little and blinds a public to the many other aspects of my work which I've struggled to cultivate: the lyrical, the paradoxical, the absurd, the ironic, the musical, the farcical and so on.

To begin – a confession: my power for invention is slight. I can invent nothing more extraordinary than what happens around me, or what I'm told happens to others. I mostly write about what I experience. The plays do not pursue what is absurd if what I've experienced does not call for the absurd. When it does call for it, I use it! Nor is irony employed when tenderness is called for; nor is the mood pervaded with lyricism if the mood requires harsh naturalism. Life comes at me too multifaceted to make a fetish of only one aspect of it; reality is too complex to be recreated in only one mould which then becomes a mannerism. I worry about writers who strait-jacket their material into personal mannerisms which are then described mistakenly as their 'voice', or their 'style'. I try to allow my material to dictate its own *inherent* style.

No doubt you will find critics and academics who do not share a view of my work as rich and varied. They may be right. After all they are wise men and women who are honoured for their wisdom by being appointed academics and critics. But no one is surprised to find a writer who believes his work *is* rich and varied. Rich and varied in what, though?

Let us try to imagine the thought process applied by academics and literary commentators to the categorizing of works of drama. You might find one who had lumped together my first five plays – *The Kitchen, The Wesker Trilogy, Chips With Everything* – in order to show how they were mainly autobiographical. Those academics might then go on to describe the next two – *Their Very Own and Golden City* and *The Four Seasons* – as being works of a metaphorical nature because the plays use strong images to represent something else: the cycle of the four seasons as a metaphor for the cycle of love coming and fading away; the failure to build the cities of our dreams as a metaphor for the compromises life forces upon us. They might then put *The Wedding Feast, Shylock,* and *Caritas* together and show how these plays had their roots in other people's stories – one based on a story by Dostoevsky called 'A Nasty Incident'; one based on the same medieval stories Shakespeare used for 'The Merchant of Venice'; the last, based on a true story about an Anchoress of the 13th Century. Or they'd put *Shylock* and *Caritas* together with *Blood Libel* and talk about them as historical plays – *Blood Libel* being about the first ever calumny of blood libel levelled at the tiny Jewish community of Norwich in 1144. They might, if they had a sense of humour, then go on to talk about 'Wesker's blue and bawdy period' citing *One More Ride on The Merry-Go Round* and *Lady Othello* – both very Rabelaisian love stories. And so on.

All that would be a possible way of looking at the work: neat groupings, tidy and orderly, packaged for study in university. But I don't think such packaging would be rewarding. Far more rewarding would be to explore the DNA of the plays; and I would propose these headings, or parts: 'Elements, subjects, themes, qualities, narrative and perceptions'. Such a breakdown might discover the work to be richer and more varied than was previously thought.

Let's look at the first of the parts – **element**. What do we mean by 'element'? I offer four examples of what I mean by 'element'. The first is 'relationship'. The basic element in all literature is relationships – lovers, friends, parent/child; oppressor/oppressed; employer/employee; brother/sister ... you can add to the list. Relationships – the first example of an 'element'.

'Nature' in literature is another example of an 'element'. Just as historians have come to recognise that geographical situation and climate affect the evolution of a people – those who live in the mountains are different from those who live by the sea, those in the cold north are different from those who live nearer the equator – so nature can affect the course of events in the unfolding of a drama. Nature – the second example of an 'element'.

I would name 'femininity' as another **element** in art. ('Masculinity', too, but I seem to have written more about women.) The feminine nature is a strong and determining factor in the telling of a tale. When discussing the feminine nature passions seethe but it can't be denied that from that first of all myths to have shaped Western civilisation – the story of Eve (the woman who knew a good thing when she saw it and courageously bit the apple of knowledge, unlike Adam who wanted to remain a good boy stuck forever in boring old paradise) – since the story of Eve the nature of femininity has been an animating **element** in all art.

'Food' is a fourth example of another element. It is said that 'we are what we eat'.

And within **element** is found **subject, theme,** and **qualities.**

Let's look at **subject** and **theme** together. I can give a simple example of what I mean by 'subject'. If a writer uses in drama the 'element' of 'femininity' then they have many choices of **subject** through which to explore this **element.** 'Mother' for example, or 'mistress', 'daughter', or 'wife'. The nature of femininity is the **element;** wife, mother, mistress or daughter is the **subject** through which femininity can be explored.

If the nature of femininity was the **element** and mother was the **subject** then we could surf through literature or drama and discover an author who has chosen to write about the mother in order to explore the **theme** of 'possessiveness', or 'jealousy', or 'love', or 'sacrifice' and so on.

Femininity is the **element**, mother is the **subject,** and sacrifice is the **theme.**

We come to **qualities.**

Qualities are to do with the method writers use to explore their **elements, subjects** and **themes.** But unfortunately, to complicate matters, there are two categories of quality: **personal quality**, and **quality of technique.**

Quality of technique is to do with the way a work is visualised, its construction, rhythm, the quality of its dialogue. The visual setting, for example, is an intrinsic part of a story, often a metaphor for the **theme.** I wrote a play called *Caritas* in which the devotional cell, where a young woman had asked to be walled up so that she could live as pure a life as possible away from the chaos of everyday life, becomes a metaphor for the prisons we all create for ourselves whether of religious belief, political ideology or marriage. Our metaphors as dramatists are part of our technique.

So, too, is the play's construction. The play needs to be constructed dynamically. The scenes or episodes within the play need to be rhythmically placed alongside each other. The dialogue demands its own kind of musicality. The way we assemble our moments, string out a character's lines – all this is to do with the **quality of technique.**

Personal quality is to do with the feelings with which a writer handles material. Qualities like humour, irony, gaiety, malice, pity. How sensitive is the writer? What **personal quality** of feeling does the writer have for their characters and their character's predicament?

Embracing, or colouring, or perhaps 'informing' is a more accurate word to use – *informing* all these first four aspects of playwriting is the fifth: **perception.**

Perception is to do with the emotional and intellectual power a writer brings to bear on the understanding of his or her material. A playwright may select an important theme, handle it with a skilful quality of technique, and paint it with an attractive personal quality of humour but *if the writer's capacity to perceive a deep truth about their theme is weak, then the work is weak.*

A writer's 'voice' is identified not by an instantly recognizable trick of dialogue but by the way their intelligence and sensitivity perceives their experience of life. We may admire technical skills but they are not what make a work of drama great enough to last through time. We may say of a writer: 'Oh, they handle dialogue so expertly, you can hear it comes out of the mouths of *real* people', but dialogue is not what carries a play across frontiers – we all know what can be lost or changed in translation. Something more is needed. Technical skills are pre-requisites; they are the *least* we expect from a playwright. It is like saying the carpenter handles his tools expertly. Yes! But is the chair beautiful to look at? And the joints may fit together with great precision but has the carpenter understood the shape and needs of the body so that the chair is comfortable to sit on?

So with the play: vibrant dialogue, effortless structure, recognizable characters, a noble theme, but how powerful is the intelligence, how sharp is the sensitivity that has informed the writer's perceptions? At what depth has human motivation been perceived? What perceptive insight has illuminated the human condition? Skills invite our admiration but perceptions touch hearts and stimulate intellect, and in such a way that they may even change our lives.

Surrounding all these aspects of writing is the last part of this DNA structure – **narrative**. The story – the framework within which we come to know the **elements, subjects, themes, qualities** and **perceptions**

THE DNA OF A PLAY

of the writer. Sometimes it is just simply the story that carries the power of the writer's perceptions.

There was a man in the land of Uz whose name was Job; and that man was perfect and upright, and one that feared God, and eschewed evil.

And God said to Satan 'look what a splendid man is my servant, Job'. To which Satan replied 'yes, but that's because you've made things easy for him. Of course he'll praise you and follow in your laws – you've blessed him with so much. But', Satan said to God:

put forth thine hand now and touch all that he hath, and he will curse thee to thy face.

And God said to Satan 'OK. Do it! I give you permission to give Job hell and see what he'll say.' And so Satan gave Job hell. But Job remained firm and faithful and God gave him back the cattle he lost and the sons and daughters Satan had caused to die.

A powerful story. Not one about an eternal truth – for we know that sometimes no matter how righteous we are, no matter how much we may please God yet we still often lose what is dear to us. But it's a marvellous biblical story about the truth of human *aspirations*. We all desire to be firm and faithful to something or other. Few of us succeed but the story of Job echoes a vivid human dream that remains on and on, a dream of the ideal person we'd all like to be.

This is a brief exploration of the question: what makes a work of art travel through time and across frontiers? Much more can be said. You can disagree with my 'DNA structure' and substitute your own parts. I've not touched on the role of language for example, that texture of prose, which can be a continuous source of delight making the work last through the centuries. But prose, as with dialogue, comes up against the problem of translation. Balzac's novels or the novels of Dostoevsky don't speak to us over the years because of the French or Russian language. Few of us speak those languages well enough. If the prose is a contributing quality making Flaubert's 'Madam Bovary' last in France it is not one to which we can lay claim in English-speaking countries or in Egypt, Turkey, China … If the novel lasts for us then we must look to identify something else, some other parts. If it is the strength of Chekhov's dialogue that make his plays constantly performed in Russia, that is not a quality we can claim in English. If Chekhov lasts for us through time then we must look for other explanations than the strength of his dialogue. And I put it to you, I suggest to you, that of all the DNA parts of a work of drama it is the writer's power of perception that carries his or her work over the centuries and across national frontiers.

4 September 1995. Reworked 1995, 1996.

3. Can playwrights be taught to write plays?

WHEN PLAYWRIGHT, DAVID Edgar, was setting up one of his seminars as head of the excellent degree course in playwriting at Birmingham University, he invited – among others, including me – fellow playwright, Timberlake Wertenbaker to participate. She accepted but expressed reservations that merit thinking about. She felt strongly that writers can best learn by just doing it. Playwrights, she thought, might do better to train as actors or stage managers so that they get to feel theatre in their bones rather than in their mind.

There is no doubt that one learns a great deal from just doing it, but having done it can 'it' be usefully commented upon? Though I've declined invitations to teach full time I have conducted short courses, and inevitably have been at the receiving end of unsolicited manuscripts. There was one instantly recognisable fault among aspiring writers that I saw could be addressed: layout. A technical feature.

I am amazed by the indifference to clarity revealed by some young writers who type huge blocks of verbose stage directions, often in CAPS so that one confronts an ugly, airless page and is almost put off going further than page three. I have on occasions re-typed a few of their pages in order to demonstrate to the aspirant how his or her play can breathe better if fewer words described character and setting. Some write dialogue with single-line spacing between the characters so that the page looks like one long speech. A clear layout is not only easier to read, it also contributes to atmosphere, mood, the rhythm of scenes. Layout can be taught. Can much more be taught?

I have given lectures 'On the Nature of Theatre Dialogue', 'On the Nature of Development.' On 'Interpretation – to explain or impose.' I have even attempted to break down 'The DNA of a play'. And when a young writer asks for advice I give them my 'Notes to Young Writers'. But do the observations handed on through those notes and lectures help to make a playwright? No one handed them on to me before I wrote my first play *The Kitchen*. Had they done so I might not have written the play because it was set in a huge restaurant kitchen for thirty-one characters. No playwriting tutor would have encouraged a young writer to write a play with such a large cast. No one in the profession thought it could work, and it was only permitted a Sunday night 'Performance Without

Décor' at The Royal Court after the success of my third play *Roots*.

But I had spent some years as an amateur actor and had even harboured ambitions for the professional stage. The ambitions never took to sea. I twice passed the entrance examinations for RADA and twice failed to obtain a grant. I had almost fulfilled one of Wertenbaker's requirements. Acting was in my bones. Even now I'm in my element giving public readings.

In June of 2004 I agreed to share the tutoring of a five day 'Advanced Playwriting Course' with Peter Rowe, artistic director of The Wolsey Theatre in Ipswich. It was organised by The Arvon Foundation, an organisation that owns three large houses around the country in which weeks are devoted to courses in writing novels, poetry, journalism, theatre, and TV drama. Students pay for board and lodging. Some – who can't afford it – obtains grants. The first house was in Devon; when the poet, Ted Hughes, died he left his Yorkshire house, Lumb Bank, to the Foundation. The late John Osborne's house in Shropshire has also been bought by Arvon and soon courses will begin there.

The atmosphere was like camping. We all made our own breakfast; the Foundation wardens, a young friendly and welcoming married couple, laid out lunch – cold meats, salads, cheese and such. In the evening students took turns in cooking the dinner – which was laid down the same each week for each course so that the 'wardens' routinely knew what to buy.

We had a good crowd ranging in age from 30s to 70s. Some married, some single, one recovering from a broken marriage – female needless to say, attractive, with two grown children, resilient.

Peter and I discussed how we were going to conduct the five days. It was agreed that we'd kick off each morning at 9.30 with me reading one of those lectures on theatre after which we'd invite the 'students' to discuss. I put 'student' in quotes because most of them were mature, some had even been performed. The rest of the time was taken up talking with them on an individual basis after reading their work.

We gave them two exercises devised by Peter: they picked out of two separate bags a slip of paper naming a couple – like 'mother and son', 'policeman and criminal', 'doctor and patient'; and from the other bag a setting – like 'a park bench', 'a doctor's surgery', 'an aeroplane', and so on. They had to write five pages of drama governed by their random picking.

Another exercise was a variation on that – we gave them the couple and the setting, 'nurse and wounded soldier at the battle front', and they each had to handle it as they wanted. An exercise that demonstrated how different writers handle the same subject. Each asked the others to read the parts for them. It was fascinating. Some were really good sketches. One young woman, a published poet who felt she'd gone as far as she could with poetry, and now wanted to experiment writing plays, was not half bad, and discovered herself to have a talent. Most had a spark but not all sparks fly afire.

I thought, as part of my tutoring, that it would be useful to read to them something of my own. After all there comes a point when the 'hints' one's trying to pass on become meaningless words requiring illustration, so one says 'here's how *I* do it'. Is that useful? After all how I 'do it' may be utterly alien to the creative spirit and rhythm of the 'student'. Arrogantly we hope our work establishes a standard.

So, a little bit of theory, some technical advice, a personal demonstration, but then one is left confronting the writer's actual work, and three things become apparent. Their dialogue is sharp, rhythmical, weighty – or it isn't! They have a sense of dramatic structure or they don't! And, most important of all, what they want to communicate has substance or it hasn't! Content is thin, ordinary, mundane. If any one of those is negative there is nothing a tutor can do to help. If the writer's ears pick up only planks of wood to reproduce dialogue that is wooden, you can't perform surgery on their ears to stop that happening. If a sense of tension or dramatic unfolding is not – as Wertenbaker would like – in their bones you can't transplant it like bone marrow. If no intellect or poetic imagination is at work you can't place it there.

I suspect that tutors of writing would like to say to many of their students 'forget it! You haven't got it!' But that is such a monstrous judgement to hurl at a would-be that most, for pity's sake, withhold. And of course they may be wrong. It may be that the writer was getting a lot of dross off his/her chest/bosom before sweet talent could surface.

In disagreeing with me some tutors might say 'our task is not to impose our rules and standards, our task is to identify what the writer is trying to achieve and help them achieve it; to identify their strengths and help make them stronger which might chase away their weaknesses.' Maybe. The problem arises when you read a work and know there is a boring mind and personality at work here. It is difficult. Rejection of one's creative output is a rejection as searing as the rejection of love. Tutoring writing involves breaking hearts. I'm not up for that.

Nevertheless I'm left with the fact that in the past over short courses I have been of help. I know it because I've been told so. What precisely is it that I've done? Peter

Rowe brings to bear his experience as a director. The writer/director relationship is at best a dynamic relationship, at worst hostile. The writer as tutor brings kinship. 'Here's a successful practitioner,' thinks the student, 'I can get close to him/her and find out how s/he does it.' Just that, I'm told, is useful enough.

Of course one offers more: comments on submitted written material; questions urging the writer to think more closely about intention, meaning, clarity, technique. The act of giving up time to be with them and take their work seriously is a source of encouragement. All that is both real and sentimental at the same time, for though the encouragement can't be denied or dismissed the reality is that mounting a play costs a lot of money, and the audience for good theatre is diminishing as curiosity to gawp at a TV or film star on stage takes over.

The teaching of the craft can't be separated from the economics of its practice. And there's worse to be confronted out there in the real world. The competition can be overwhelming. Everyone, it seems, wants to be a writer. For the serious writer the warriors to confront are legion: Bond, Pinter, Hare, Bennett, Edgar, Churchill, Frayn, Shaffer, Harwood, and Wertenbaker et al, to say nothing of the new discoveries like Ravenshill, Harris, Greig, Butterworth, Craig and the late Kane, plus.

And last, there is the nature of the director who may or may not be in tune with what the writer is endeavouring to communicate. Let me end with a salutary anecdote. I was recently invited by the Union of Swedish Playwrights to deliver my lecture on 'Interpretation', about the tensions that can exist between playwright and director. A panel of professionals discussed with the public what I'd said. One of the panellists was a young director who revealed that when she finished training she was advised not to start her career with a new play because then more attention would be given to the play than her production. You can't teach a young playwright how to handle that.

19 April 2005, Blaendigeddi

4. Interpretation – to impose or explain.

a defence of meaning

in

three Acts, a Prologue and an Epilogue

Preamble

SOME INTERPRETERS ARE greater at interpreting than some creators are at creating. However, roughly and provocatively speaking:

actors and directors tend to say: look at me

writers say: listen to me

actors and directors tend to call upon an audience to admire performance and spectacle

writers invite an audience to be thoughtful about experience, and to feel deeply

the craft of the actor and director tends more to engage ego, and is therefore a limited activity

the art of the writer engages vision, and is therefore resonant

actors and directors make decisions involving craft and emotion

writers make decisions involving craft, emotion and intellect actors and directors risk their reputations for skills, what they can *do*

writers risk their reputations for perceptions and the values held, *who* they are

An ongoing debate in British theatre is centred on the fear that performance, i.e. what the director and actor offer, is taking over, as the basis of theatrical creation from text, i.e. what the playwright offers. I am going to address this problem in three Acts, a Prologue and an Epilogue.

The 'Prologue' will consist of a quote from Harold Pinter and a short poem by Berthold Brecht translated by John Willet.

In Act One I will explore the *nature of 'interpretation'.* In Act Two I will explore a distinction between *showbiz and art.* All of which should come together in Act Three, which will be a *Defence of Words.* The Epilogue will be *a story.*

Prologue

"It is certainly an inventive production. Signor Visconti has in fact invented a new play, where major, significant and quite crucial pieces of action are introduced into a play by the director, without consultations with the author ... I did not write a play about two lesbians who caress each other continually. I did not write a scene in which a woman exposes herself to a man on stage. There is nothing in the text to indicate that the man and woman powder the naked breasts of the wife on stage. I did not write a musical. The characters sing songs but I did not state that a piano should accompany them, nor that the piano should continue in the most widely inappropriate places. All the sexual acts I have referred to are not only inexpressibly vulgar in themselves but are totally against the spirit and intention ... Let me remind you that a play is not a public property. It belongs to its author under the international law of copyright."

Harold Pinter, publicly commenting on Visconti's production of
Old Times *in the Teatro di Roma*

Plays and Players – a poem by Berthold Brecht

The play is over. The performance committed. Slowly
The theatre, a sagging intestine, empties. In the dressing
rooms
The nimble salesmen of hotchpotch mimicry, of rancid
rhetoric
Wash off make-up and sweat. At last
The lights go down which showed up the miserable
Botched job; twilight falls on the
Lovely nothingness of the misused stage. In the empty
Still mildly smelly auditorium sits the honest
Playwright, unappeased, and does his best
To remember.

Act One – a brief exploration
of the nature of 'interpretation'.

THE PROBLEM OF what should happen when a director accepts to realise on the stage what has been written on the page – a process that is often called interpretation – is a complex problem and one that raises principles of fundamental ethical importance.

There can be no doubt that in the last 70 years directors have emerged who have changed the visual, audio and choreographic experience of the theatre. My own experiences of working with directors is mixed. The worst have lead to changes to which I should never have agreed, and resulted in disaster; the best have been rewarding and resulted in changes to text and structure which have enhanced the power and meaning of the play. But –

– a madness is sweeping through world theatre, a madness that has elevated the role and importance of the director above the role and importance of the playwright. The stage has become shrill with the sounds of the director's vanity; it has become cluttered with his or her tricks and visual effects. No play is safe from their, often hysterical, manipulations. The productions we are seeing claim attention to themselves rather than to the play. The playwright's vision of the human condition has become secondary to the director's bombastic striving for personal impact; the playwright's text, the playwright's visual concepts, his rhythmic arrangement of scenes, her emotional tensions, his unfolding of narrative action, her perceptions of human behaviour, are distorted, re-arranged, cut, or ignored by the director and sometimes by the actors.

Let us remind ourselves of something that is perhaps forgotten. The raw material of the playwright is their individual experience of life. This experience is a kind of chaos into which occasionally there shines a light, a tiny light of meaning. A small part of the chaos is identified, sometimes comprehended. Playwrights give this comprehended chaos a shape, an order; they call it a play. And like scholars they are handling what are called primary sources, which no one else has explored. Those primary sources are their own being and experience for which an original quality of imagination, and a kind of courage is called upon because they are going where no one dared to go before.

The metamorphosis which seems to be taking place in the theatre is this: directors are usurping plays as *their* primary source, as *their* raw material to do with it as they fancy. The playwright *endures* the life and from it shapes a play; the director often rapes it.

The difference between the playwright and director is usually defined in terms of function – the playwright writes, the director enables what has been written to be performed. I don't believe mere function adequately describes the difference. For me the most important difference between the two of them is that whereas the playwright commits his private being to public exposure, at the end of a production you know of a director only the degree of their talent for organising spectacle, and their skill for orchestrating performance and movement on stage. Occasionally a text is clarified. But you end knowing nothing about their private life, their fears or self-doubts, and little of the quality of their thought, their poetic powers of perception. They have not committed or risked ambivalences, uncertainties, they have not articulated views which go against the cant in vogue, you do not know in detail what the director thinks about sex, politics, or human beings in the way you know what writers think and feel after they have written their plays. And in exercising their power the director seems to be supported by critics and academics, and, finally, the audience; playwrights are relegated to the role of innocent children needing the stern hand of a father, a fuehrer, to control and guide them.

My own view is that this power, like the power of the bully, has grown out of a deep sense of inadequacy. The creative artist takes exhilarating risks either by handling explosive material or daring to think, utter, record, describe what few others dare, and to identify what no one has before identified. Directors, understandably but mistakenly, often feel lacking by comparison with what they have to offer; and because they can't repaint da Vinci, or re-write *Crime and Punishment*, or publish Dante's *Inferno* to be read back to front; because they can't put the choral part of Beethoven's 9th symphony in the beginning or middle instead of at the end, so they turn to theatre. There is something about the process of rehearsing a play which, requiring the physical presence of a director, encourages them to slip in and indulge what it excites and flatters them to call their 'concepts' at the expense of the playwright's vision. The playwright's work can be distorted, even censored, and no one objects. When it is a new play no one even knows. It is considered to be legitimate directorial interpretation.

Don't misunderstand me. I am not suggesting that every creative writer is a genius. Many are mediocre. If the creative artist can be described as dealing in perceptions then it must be conceded that many writers either *mis*-perceive or deal in dreary perceptions. For this reason all art must be open to questioning and criticism. But I am here trying to identify an *extreme* development in the theatre, one in which it is automatically assumed either that all new playwriting is faultily constructed, erroneously perceived and therefore a director or an actor can do to a new play what they like; or the work is viewed as a kind of fertile little plot of land into which director and actor can transplant their own saplings in the name of 'self expression'. Little humility exists among the interpreters. So extreme is this development that directors are refusing to direct the plays of living playwrights or plays that are tightly constructed leaving no room for them to impose their 'concepts'.

Another lecture could be spun around two other relevant but complex questions. First: reasonable arguments can be offered for revamping established, classical plays, though the question cannot be avoided: is not a classic new for *some*one in the audience and therefore a so-called 'interpretation' could easily distort and deny the classical playwright's intentions for that person for whom the experience is a first? I confess, I'd like to direct a very trimmed version of T*he Merry Wives of Windsor* to reveal the dark play that's lost in all the ho-ho heartiness of the piece, but I would not pretend I was serving the Bard.

Second: many artists reject the notion that they are creating. Everyone, they observe, is claiming the right and the talent to be 'creative' but only God (or whoever) is creative, the rest of us are engaged in *re*-creating; re-creating our experience of life, which process could itself be described as a kind of interpretation. If the writer, therefore, is interpreting, what is it that directors and actors are doing – interpreting an interpretation? Is this possible?

Another question: whose *is* the voice primarily we go to hear in the theatre? We surely don't want to hear all the voices together, do we? We don't want the stage to become like a meeting room in which everyone is shouting at the same time so that we do not know who is saying what; isn't it important when we are watching a play to know whether we are hearing the playwright's voice, the actor's, the director's, or the set designer's?

Theatre people often behave as though theirs was the only art form in the world. It is not. Theatre's art is merely one of many. And just as painting is not primarily about paintbrushes or the nature of paint, as music is not about violins or the violinist, as novels are not about printing-machines or publishers, so theatre is not about actors, directors or empty spaces. Theatre, like all art, is about, or to do with, life; to be precise – the artist's perceptions about life. *That*, when I read a poem, or a novel, or look at a painting or listen to music is the voice I want to hear. And that too is what I want to hear and understand when I go to the theatre: the

voice of the playwright formulating his or her perceptions about life. The playwright is a fool who does not
acknowledge debts to the team that helps his play to
the stage, but theatres do not exist for the convenience
of stage-hands or the greater glory of the actor, director,
designer or critic, delighted though we may be when
that glory has been earned. The audience's *raison d'être*
for attending theatre is the play. The *raison d'être* for the
theatre team is to mount that play for an audience as its
intentions can best be realised.

"Oh," cry the actor and director, "what about *my*
voice, my right to say something, what about *my* point
of view? Am I not intelligent? Don't I too have perceptions about life? I may even have more interesting
perceptions about life than you the writer."

Perfectly true! They *have* rights, and they *may* have
more interesting perceptions. But what is the most
honest way to exercise those rights, to present those
perceptions? Does a director have the right to re-
arrange or to cut a writer's text so that the play is no
longer communicating what the playwright wishes to
communicate but instead is communicating what the
director wishes to communicate? Imagine that I have
created the character of an unfaithful wife shaping her
to be presented as gentle, bewildered, and demanding
of our pity. Has an actress the right to present that

unfaithful wife on stage as a ruthless woman because *she* thinks unfaithful wives are ruthless women?

Let us for a moment accept the moral right of the director and the actor to interpret in the sense of imposing their own views, making their own comment, delivering the lines with the emphasis and melody *they* think the lines *ought* to have. Let us assume an audience has given them the right. The director, you say, is an artist like Mr Wesker, and we want to know the director's point of view. But his point of view on what?

If we are in a room discussing 'what' then you would say: Mr Wesker, you speak first, let's hear *your* voice, and then we want to know and will listen to what the director has to say. That would be just, reasonable, you will have heard my point of view. It would also be the most practical method of procedure; the alternative would be a tower of Babel – everyone talking at the same time. But if the director is imposing his views in a stage-production by cutting text, re-arranging the sequence of events, placing the action in a setting different from what the playwright has imagined; and if the actress is interpreting the unfaithful wife as a ruthless woman rather than rendering her a gentle, bewildered woman, then how will you know what it was that the playwright *wanted* to say? In the room you asked to *hear* the play-wright's voice. On stage you have no control and the playwright's voice has been *suppressed*. How, then, can you evaluate the validity of the director's and actor's point of view if you haven't been allowed to hear, and therefore do not know, what they are having a point of view about?! And what about the sheer rudeness of it all? Imagine the fury of a director if a rehearsal was called by the playwright or another director who began to change the shape of his or her production. Imagine the playwright or someone leaping on to the stage and pushing the actor aside saying, no! this is how I meant it to be done. When a playwright's intention is ignored or distorted then that is what is happening – he or she is being rudely pushed aside. Worse, when another voice muffles theirs then it becomes an act of censorship and in democratic societies that is unacceptable.

So, how can the actress exercise her right to comment? Well, there are three ways perhaps. First she can decide not to perform the role because she is out of sympathy with it; and she can then look for a play in which the unfaithful wife *is* presented as ruthless. *That* becomes her comment. Or she can talk with the playwright first and try to persuade him he is wrong and that she is right. Or she can write her own play. The right she does not have is to accept to play the role and then to play it in a way that is against the spirit and intention of the playwright.

The same scenario can be written for the director. He has the right to accept or not accept to direct a play, to discuss his views with the playwright, to look for another play or to write his own play. And all this of course is precisely what is happening. Actors, frustrated by the tyranny of directors, and feeling they have perceptions they wish to illustrate on stage, are devising their own productions. Directors, feeling strait-jacketed by a playwright's vision, are turning playwright. And playwrights, feeling their work misunderstood by directors, are taking the clay into their own hands and sculpting their works. I see all this as right and proper and not divisive. I am here not to argue against actors and directors becoming playwrights, or devisors of theatrical happenings, but to explain the playwright's function as I see it and to argue for my preference which, finally is language, not exclusively but predominantly; and I say this as the author who placed 31 actors in the setting of a kitchen where action and movement is virtually non-stop, and who from then on constantly sought telling visual settings for most of his subsequent plays.

Nor do I want to give the impression that when I finish writing a play at my desk then that is the last word, nothing can be changed. On the contrary, I need to listen to everybody's comments: family's, friends', director's, actors', set-designer's. I owe many changes to them all. Mostly I like to direct my own plays because then I can speak directly with the actors without that dread which playwrights are driven to feel that any observations they make about their own play might undermine the authority of the director. An absurd situation in which the director's dignity is more important than clarification of the playwright's intentions!

Act Two – a distinction
between Showbiz and Art.

A DISTINCTION BETWEEN SHOWBIZ and art needs to be identified in order that a playwright be given freedom to develop. Freedom to develop and explore new areas of their power is essential; the one characteristic we deplore in any artist is opportunism. But for perfectly understandable reasons the market-place invites opportunism: investors do not want to lose money, subsidised theatres cannot sustain endless deficits, and directors must be – in this precarious, unholy trade – constantly on the lookout for opportunities of glory and wealth. Herein lies the playwright's central dilemma: on the one hand slow, painstaking development with all its risks and attendant condemnations; on the other hand opportunism with its instant applause and the chance to survive.

A further phenomenon obtrudes: a neurotic, anal urge by academics and media to divide life into decades. The best writers work at material they believe is of lasting value. They may be self-deluded and be writing ephemera – posterity will judge that – but serious artists work in the belief that they are selecting material on the basis of criteria that will cross time and frontiers, that they are contributing to a mainstream of drama going back to the beginning, and not the current vogue of a mere ten years.

Of course Euripides belongs to 5th century BC Greece, and Shakespeare to 16th century England, and Chekhov to pre-revolutionary Russia, but something other than the decade or the century marks them: a strange chemistry made up of perceptive intelligence, poetic sensibility, imagination and God knows what, that enables these writers both to reflect *and* to stamp their times with a quality of insight from which future generations seem able continually to refresh themselves. No writer attempts to *calculate* how this can be achieved, they write as they must. Lasting impact is, however, what all writers *hope* they have achieved. Whether I have succeeded or not I don't know but I do know that I never contemplate material unless I feel it can resonate, unless I sense that it's more than itself.

The English fight shy of the concept of the 'artist'. To consider oneself an artist is to 'take on airs'. A bit pretentious actually. Few in the theatre dare or quite know how to make the distinction between the lovely lady everyone loves to love called 'showbiz' and the embarrassing slut everyone wishes stayed away called 'art'. The result is that criteria become jumbled and inverted snobbery reigns.

It is not an easy distinction to handle. Few in Britain enjoy being caught 'serious' for fear they might be thought 'solemn'. It is cosier and more comforting to link arms with the multitude and 'have a good night out'. The possibility that 'a good night out' can be achieved through engagement with intellect, emotion and laughter at a level richer than 'the multitude' is normally considered capable of, is deemed haughty, snooty, high-and-mighty, bumptious, imperious, high-brow, egg-head, high-falutin', arty-farty, airy-fairy – Roget's Thesaurus is full of the dismissive jargon fed to the fond multitude. The contempt showbiz moguls really have for the poor multitude is an essay in itself. It has remained a mystery to me that with everything going for them – vast financial backing and popular success – showbiz requires such a savage arsenal of insults for those of us huddled together in remote corners really unwanted if the truth be told, our heads hung low muttering, despite the terrorism of showbiz demagogues, 'yes, well, actually, we *are* artists. Sorry about that'.

But what *is* the distinction between art and showbiz? The question is almost a philosophical one and cannot be answered satisfactorily in a brief essay such as this. It has to do with three elements: with the complexity of the material handled, with the power of thought brought to bear upon that material, and with the degree of poetry applied to the play's conception. None of the great and basic themes are simple to handle – love, death, meaning, old age, happiness, self-contempt, disillusion – even the stuff of laughter. Some laughs are cheap, easily earned; others are rich, hard-earned. And by complexity I do not mean obscurity. The demand of art is for as much clarity and simplicity as possible. But life and living are not simple and sometimes no matter how hard an artist strives for clarity and simplicity it cannot always be approached because the material is Gordian, the going hard.

There is also this: art finally is a passionate, individual vision tailored for no one in particular. It is one person's view of the world. Showbiz cannot be expected to accommodate this. The stakes are too high. The public's taste and needs are all. Ambitious directors will sacrifice the individual vision and tailor it to what is imagined is the public's taste. I do not quarrel with this nor stand in judgement. My plea as always is for distinctions to be made.

Act Three – Defence of The Word.

I'VE READ MY plays around the world at theatre festivals to which many wordless productions have travelled from festival to festival, put together with the intention of appealing across the language barrier of audiences anywhere. They were 'devised' sometimes by the entire group or assembled from the imagination of the director. Their quality has varied from the imaginative to the banal, the witty to the cliché, the lyrical to the pretentious – image straining after image to say something without words. One question hangs over them all: what or how much can be said without words?

At a certain level the question is redundant, even foolish, since three out of the four great art forms are wordless: music, dance, painting and sculpture. We can ask *this* question however: what exactly is it that music – to take the most popular of the wordless arts – can say without words? Or rephrased: what *can't* it say?

Music cannot utter the words 'I love you'. But that does not matter because notes can form a moving equivalent. Music cannot utter the words 'I am depressed by human behaviour'. That, too, does not matter since music can create a disturbing equivalent for that sentiment. Can music recreate the tension between good and evil which literature deals with in great detail? The answer must be yes to that, too, though not in as great a detail nor, obviously, in detail of the same kind. So what *exactly* is it that music cannot do?

Human beings seem to progress through life helped by the exercise of thought and emotion. Music can handle emotion, it cannot handle thought. Let me clarify that statement. Music may not be able to *handle* thought but the composition of music *engages* thought. The composer must be thoughtful *about* music. Also music can excite emotions to such depths that the emotion *prompts* profound thoughts, but no composer would employ notes to argue a philosophical concept. I know of no passage of orchestral music that confronts me with the question 'To be or not to be'. Nor can musical notes go on to present the specific arguments Hamlet works out for himself before deciding *whether* to be or not to be. We do not turn to music for the exploration of such distressing dilemmas.

I am identifying differences not establishing orders of merit – my life is inconceivable without music which I listen to more than I watch theatre, and personally I would prefer to have been a composer working in the abstract forms of music rather than in the contentious and murky waters of drama where thought can be argued with. Few think they can compose a better symphony than the composer, but many more think they can write a better play than the playwright. The point I am making is that if we want to experience art without words we turn to music, ballet, painting and sculpture. Theatre is the home of language and thought, and in these days when TV screams bullets, terror and one-liner comedies at us, and the boards of most theatres bounce with musicals then language and thought are at a premium.

The absence of thought is my quarrel with those new forms of drama mushrooming around the world. The visual aspect is only a part of the theatrical experience. Stage design, action, movement, physical imagery have their place on stage but as aids rather than a central force. I am not so purist that I cannot accept the idea of ballet employing words; nor will I turn from using music in a play – though music in drama worries me, it is such an emotive art that I fear it becoming a crutch to support crippled substance; nor would I decry a form of drama that marries music, dance and the spoken word in a form other than the ubiquitous musical. But language is the only tool humans have forged to conceptually identify and define experience, and the theatrical impact that lingers for me is when characters have locked into conflicts or celebrations through the dynamic of the spoken word.

To be or not to be, that is the question.
Whether 'tis nobler in the mind to suffer
The slings and arrows of outrageous fortune
Or to take arms against a sea of troubles
And by opposing, end them?

In the English of Shakespeare are combined three strengths: an exciting musical sound made by words; a collection of metaphors which illuminate our lives – *the slings and arrows of outrageous fortune;* a power of thought which identifies a dilemma we confront each day: do we battle with bureaucracy, fools, incompetence, indifference, malevolence, or turn a blind eye to them and maintain a dignified silence? Theatre without words cannot engage us at such a complex level.

I know that language has limitations and can spread confusion as easily as it can clarify, but despite all the abuse to which language is prone it is the most extraordinary piece of equipment forged by humans for their better understanding of themselves, one another and the world in which they live.

I warm to abstract art, whether on canvas, in stone, or in architecture; but I cannot sit through two or three hours of abstract drama where characters without words speak to me only in simple terms. I am a complex being in a complex world. I require the power of words to formulate thoughts that help me stumble through a complex life. Theatre-without-words tells me only that spring can bring joy, that kindness can melt hard hearts, that all we need is love, that war is evil. It cannot detail the conflicts of interest that lead to war so that I can make judgements, nor can it heart-achingly explain why war sometimes may be needed to combat evil. Theatre that tries to communicate simple thoughts in images or action without language is finally a theatre of primary emotions. At its best theatre-without-words may arouse admiration for skill and imagination, at its worst it may mislead by omission, and in leaving out so much risks dishonesty. In spreading thin its specificity it becomes kindergarten theatre.

Epilogue – a story.

A T A FRIEND'S house for dinner one night were assembled some eminent directors and equally eminent playwrights. I think my host guessed the frisson that might occur. Inevitably the conversation centred on the differences that grow between writer and director during rehearsals. One writer, whose fame is international and who was not English, finally confessed in words more or less as follows:

(With a New England accent)

"My problem is that I rarely encounter a director whose theatrical imagination is more interesting than mine." Gasps and superior smiles followed. He continued: "They're full of gimmicks and deceits and technical effects which are childish and banal. I'm very puritanical. You have to earn what you make an audience feel, not use technology and tricks for short cuts and manipulation. All my carefully constructed rhythms of speech are ignored, evolving emotional tensions are lost and rendered feeble, the reasons for juxtaposing scene to scene, the relevance of certain physical actions, the call for specific props, colours, textures, my metaphors, none of it is understood. I want to give up and write novels".

One of the directors, who is on record as saying he prefers to work with dead playwrights (as some playwrights might wish they were working with dead directors?) asked:

"But what about objectivity? How many playwrights do you know who've ever been objective about their work?"

Our un-English playwright responded by asking the same question: "How many directors do you know who've ever been objective about their productions?"

The director pressed ahead.

"And what a statement of massive arrogance to say you've never encountered a director whose theatrical imagination was more interesting than yours".

At which the playwright descended into what I can only describe as speechless bewilderment.

"But surely," he struggled to articulate, "when a director insists upon changes in my play isn't he declaring that *his* theatrical imagination is more interesting than *mine*?"

The rest of us writers said nothing to all this, fearing for our futures perhaps. What remained with me was the foolhardy writer's look of utter bewilderment. It was the double standard had rendered him speechless.

The director said: "Well, I couldn't ever work on one of your plays that's for sure. You'd leave me nothing to say".

At which the by now miserable visiting playwright exploded and, I suspect, subsequently regretted his explosion:

"But I don't write my fucking plays to enable you to say anything. Make your own boat to travel in. I spend sometimes two years constructing my boat, I don't want you cutting fancy holes in the side so that the water comes in and all you have to do is hop on some other poor playwright's boat and wave goodbye while I sink to the bottom".

"There, there!" said another of the directors, "one of us might come along and rescue you one day. And think of all the plays you could write on the desert island which of course you'll manage to swim to because we all know you're a survivor".

"I can't fucking swim," muttered the defeated playwright, "that's why I build fucking boats".

But by this time English mockery had once again saved the evening. Everyone laughed.

This essay is, I'm aware, contentious. Let me end on a note of harmony. I have derived too much pleasure from the work of directors, and from working with actors to want to see us at each other's throats. The possibility of conflict is ever present in the arts. Egos are large, vulnerability runs deep, delight in downfall waits malevolently in the wings. But conflict is not inevitable. If a group of actors want to create a work together that offers more physical action than text – why not? If a director wants to take a dead playwright's text and reassemble it in his own image – why not, the original text is always there. If an ensemble wants to use dance, mime, slides, music – the entire potent, technical armoury at the disposal of theatre – why not? But if I want to write a play in which the excitement resides in the way characters are animated by their thoughts and emotions to actually talk – I would like to think that those in power (for let us be absolutely clear about this, the writer has no power, it has been handed to the director) I would like to think that those in power will also say – why not? For remember – the best playwrights conceive their plays with images, sound and movement as well as text.

Sooner or later pockets of power must be offered to the playwright, otherwise the only theatre we will experience is that which the director permits us to experience. In Britain we have many playwrights who also direct their own plays. Not every playwright wishes or is temperamentally suited to do so. But I would like to see encouraged the emergence of a new breed of playwright/director. Not an exclusive breed (we should not rise to the bait of divisiveness) simply an additional breed, to enrich the scene.

I rest my case.

Originally written in 1988, updated 24 February 2010

5. *From Stage to Page – thoughts on the difference between writing plays and novels.*

I DISCOVERED THE DIFFERENCE between the two crafts to be numerous. The novel was more difficult to control. A play is like a race horse, just one bridle to hold. The novel is a huge wagon pulled by many horses – more words, more characters, more settings. You can't get away with the simplistic in a novel as you can in a play; on the other hand you can take your time in a way that you can't in the theatre.

In both forms the writer can make an emotional impact, but when theatre is at its best that emotional impact can be visceral as prose can't be because it is humans talking to humans, not print talking to humans. The downside is that the human voice of the actor dictates how the written voice is received. A virtue of the novel is that, without the actor as intermediary, readers are given freedom to build their own picture of events and personalities. The novelist trusts his readers to 'get it' without help. More, the printed work allows a reader to go back over a paragraph not understood first time round. It could be said that: the stage dictates, the page liberates.

Honey is about one of the characters, Beatie Bryant, in my early play, *Roots*, the second in *The Wesker Trilogy*. *Roots* ends with Beatie, the daughter of a farm labourer, discovering her own voice. The question was often asked: what happened to Beatie after she discovered her own voice? For a long time I wanted to answer that question, and always knew it would be in the form of a novel. It could have been a play but the material as it mulled around in my head always suggested itself as material for a novel. That form would provide a larger canvas for more subtle thoughts and interplay. Added to which I have always wanted to write a novel.

I grew up on novels not plays. Though I wanted to be an actor we could not afford the theatre. The Odeon cinema in Brick Lane was where I honed a sense of drama. The only plays I saw were those I acted in as an amateur in Toynbee Hall at Aldgate East. Life and ideas came to me through the novel.

Novels were sagas of simple beginnings which grew in complexity, unfolded compellingly as characters made decisions that damaged their lives or lead them to impact upon each other in sometimes happy, sometimes disastrous, ways. They wrung me out whether written by D.H Lawrence or A.J. Cronin; Upton Sinclair or

Dostoevsky, Howard Spring or George Orwell. I panicked if there was not another Penguin to hand to be picked up after I'd finished reading the previous one. I lived each page intensely and marvelled at the writer's skill and power of perception. I wanted to move other people as those writers had moved me.

My first attempt (inexplicably titled '*Dorna Karshon*') was made when I was about twelve; begun but never finished. My second attempt, very bad, was based on the experience of National Service in the RAF, which I later turned into a play called *'Chips With Everything'*. And though my career went into writing plays (and four books of short stories along the way) I kept over the years a box file called 'Notes towards a novel', full of scribbled-on sheets; and later a computer file of 'first lines'. Three examples of first lines that didn't lead anywhere:

His suicide note read: "Sorry, darlings, I couldn't work it out." This is the story of what it was he could not work out.

'Bury the body and remember the good times' – those were his last words. **What** *good times?*

The restaurant was quiet with careful couples carefully chewing their meals and not conversing.

Forty-two plays later the novel-writing mood descended, and a 'first line' (which had grown into a paragraph) dated 6th May 1997 flew afire.

He said: "When you get too old for it, like me, you look. I'm sorry, young woman. Rude of me. I've finished my coffee. I'm going."

I told him I didn't mind. "Men always look at me" I said. "I'm beautiful." That made him smile, and in his smile I saw the young man he once was and thought – the streets are full of young men trapped in old men's bodies.

That seemed promising, and I felt driven to fan the flames into a novel.

I knew the experience of writing a novel would be – to change metaphors – a bumpy ride of pitfalls and surprises. I recorded the journey as a diary. One of the reasons for writing a novel rather than a play was, I wrote in that diary, *'to free myself from the interpretations of concept-crazy directors who want to intrude their voice into the play as though the writer's voice was inadequate.'* The stage filters the playwright through director, actor and sometimes designer. The novel's page allowed me to speak directly to my reader.

The biggest difference therefore, it must be confessed, was to do with control. I wanted greater control of my material. I listen to comments and advice but I need to know I have final control because in the end it's my head that rolls. If I want to present an unfaithful wife on the stage as gentle, bewildered, demanding of our pity then I don't want an actress presenting her as a ruthless woman because she, the actress, thinks unfaithful wives are ruthless women.

Many would say that such filtering is needed because it tempers the 'God-like' authorial voice. Of late that voice has been attacked for its deistic presumptions, but the thrill of reading those novels of my youth lay in that very individual, idiosyncratic, 'God-like' voice. The ultimate power of all free art is that the 'God-like' voice is only a temporary one. When you have put the book down you can argue with, and measure – from your own experience – what 'God' has observed and perceived, and accept it or reject it.

It will be obvious that *Honey* was written by a playwright because there is more dialogue than description; my novel doesn't begin with: *'It was a dark and stormy night'* but with: *'He said'*. For me people describe themselves through what they say and the *tone* of what they say as well as their actions. Have I achieved a crossover? Others must decide. Despite that I thrill to the spoken word, dialogue as opposed to descriptive prose, I hope that where descriptive prose was called for I rose to it.

17 September 2005

6. The Nature of Development

MY LECTURE WILL be in three parts. In the first part I'd like to put to you an observation I put before audiences whenever I can. It's to do with categories. There appears to exist a need on the part of critics and audiences neatly to label an artist's work. The need exists because it's thought that the labelling will help *understand* the artist's work. '... Oh, he's an absurdist, he's an naturalist, she's a social realist ...' Wise, knowing nods, little more left to say. The need to label is understandable but the labels supplied are often unhelpful, distorting. I'd like you for a moment to forget all such categorising and to consider instead the following observation as possibly a more helpful and – to my mind – more accurate guide to the understanding of an artist's work.

No art is realistic. The concept of 'realistic art' is a concept involving contradictions. No play or story I've ever written can usefully or truthfully be described as a 'realistic' play or story. The recreation of total reality in any artistic medium is impossible. It's even impossible to *experience* total reality, reality being the sum total of an infinite number of moments. For example, sit in a room with people and you realise that you can't experience the reality of that situation because you can't see the back of their heads, you can't see their legs under that table, you don't know what they're thinking.

Now, if that seems so obvious as to be too foolish to state then it's because the concept of 'realistic art' is itself foolish. However, although there is no such phenomenon as 'realistic art' it is quite interesting and helpful to observe that all art *deals* with the experience of reality. From here on we can begin to make useful categories. We can now say an artist is dealing with what is absurd in reality, what is paradoxical in reality, or ironic or mystical or commanding of our pity. And we may add that the artist is dealing with what is absurd in reality *in a naturalistic form*, or that the artist is dealing with naturalistic aspects of reality *in an absurd form* – the permutations are extensive. Once it is accepted that reality is the anchor to all art then the categories are less divisive, and an image emerges of all artists wrestling with the same problems of identifying and illuminating their experience of it. The common 'enemy' is the reality of the chaos of our existence and different artists choose to deal with it in different ways.

Why am I at such pains to re-identify the categories? Because I think false links and misguided assumptions of merit will be made if identification is inaccurate. For example, once we accept that all art deals with an artist's experience and perception of reality then we might find that Beckett's experience and perception has more in common with Chekhov's than with, say, Ionesco's, though Beckett and Ionesco have been categorised as absurdists, and Chekhov as a naturalist. Such categories are divisive and tell us nothing, and what we should be looking for are not our cosy, divisive categories but *the power of the artist's perception of reality*. Is it a powerful or feeble perception of reality? After all feebleness of vision can emerge no matter in what *form* the artist constructs his work. A writer who has chosen to explore what is absurd or chosen an absurd form to explore what is naturalistic is quite likely to be a superficial observer with feeble powers of perception; just as a writer who has chosen a naturalistic form to explore social injustice may have some very dull and undistinguished views *about* that social injustice. It's the quality of vision, the perception of reality, their values which create the true affinities and divisions between artists, not their forms. Too often a public enjoys the work of a writer whose form they happen to be in love with in that decade.

John Ruskin, the great Victorian art critic who rescued one of our finest painters from the attacks of the critics of the day, said this of Turner. That in Turner's lifetime:

> ... when people first looked at him, those who liked rainy weather said he was not equal to Copley Fielding; but those who looked at Turner long enough found that he could be much more wet than Copley Fielding when he chose. The people who liked force said that Turner was not strong enough for them; he was effeminate; they liked De Wint – nice strong tone; – or Cox – great, greeny dark masses of colour – solemn feeling of the freshness and depth of nature; they liked Cox – Turner was too hot for them. Had they looked long enough they would have found that he had far more force than De Wint, far more freshness than Cox <u>when he chose</u>, only united with other elements; and that he didn't choose to be cool, if nature had appointed the weather to be hot ... And so throughout with all thoroughly great men, their strength is not seen at first, precisely because they united, in due place and measure, every great quality ...

It was necessary to undermine that need to categorize before talking about what I feel to be the problem of my own development, because it's certain that – for those of you who have thought about my work at all – you

will have thought about it based upon the careless cate-
gorizations of journalists, or the not always adequately
informed observations of over-worked academics. I
wanted it fully appreciated that I shared, in common
with *all* artists, the function of exploring and identifying reality. It means nothing to think of my plays and
stories as social realism – a term I've grown to resent
because it blinds people to those other elements in my
work I'd always hoped would be recognized: the paradoxical, the lyrical, the absurd, ironic, musical, farcical
and so on; all the elements united, as Ruskin says, in
'due place and measure'.

In the second part I'd like to break down the elements
of a stage play in order to see *where* there is room for
development, where *exactly* can one look for it. What
are the elements of a stage play?

There's *space*: the relationship of action to audience;
there's *setting*, or design if you like; there's *performer*;
there's *sound;* and finally – *text*. I doubt if these elements
have ever changed. Even a performance from a wagon
in medieval times employed those same elements. Space
was used; not our elaborate twentieth-century theatres,
but from wagon to street level. Setting was used; not
our expensive costumes and props, or our moving plat-
forms and complex lighting systems, true, but a cut-
out tree here or a wooden sword there. There was

performer; not our highly trained and theory-ridden actors of today, but an extrovert spirit of sorts. There was sound; not the electronic sounds we can assemble on tape but a drum or two, a flute or two; and there was text – perhaps an element that was of greater distinction then than now, certainly by the time we reached Shakespeare. And there's hardly a permutation of those elements that hasn't been used: with or without costume, with or without set, with daylight or lamplight, in proscenium, in the round, on multi-stages, or with action going on in the audience's lap!

Nor can it be claimed that the greater degree of technical sophistication has encouraged a significant development in the quality of theatre writing. I doubt if the mere existence of a magnificent National Theatre will produce a Shakespeare. Even the elements in the structure of text have remained the same: there has been verse, lyrical prose, lyrical naturalism, colloquial and absurd dialogue. Each writer in a generation or wave *may* have learned how to respond to the textural sound and rhythmic needs of the day but does any such response signify 'development'? Woe betide the dramatist writing in verse when street-corner conversations are thought to reflect the dynamic of contemporary encounters. But does the dramatist who catches street-corner rhythms merit the description 'developed'? Is that all that is needed? A tuned ear is the least basic tool we expect in a dramatist.

Or should we look to the framework within which the text lives? But that, likewise, has been thoroughly explored: dozens of scenes and different settings in Elizabethan drama, the one-act play, the two-act, three-act play, each act with one or two or ten scenes, the play with one set and a few characters, the play with thirty sets and thirty characters ... Whatever the permutations the basic elements have remained. And to move from a traditional three-act drama to a multi-scened one may involve a degree of courage but can that be described as 'development'? Isn't that rather a 're-arrangement'? The playwright may have found the courage to take on more complex *technical* challenges but he may be applying that complex structure to say the same things. The technical flurries may be very intoxicating and thrilling in themselves but they can very easily be hiding a trite or uninteresting observation about human behaviour. You must be very careful with theatre people, they have tricks they can use to make you *think* you're experiencing something profound when in fact you're not. They can turn on the heat and make you *feel* strongly about absolutely nothing at all. In the wrong hands it can become a mere masturbatory art!

So, since they've always been there, a change around of the *physical elements* can only properly be described as a rearrangement. No dramatist can be viewed as having developed merely by re-arranging or re-structuring his form *unless that re-arranging corresponds to a similar process in his perception of his experience of reality.* Which brings me to the third and final part in which I'd like to look a little more closely at this last element – the artist's perception of the reality of his experience. When one has broken down a play into its physical parts, as I have tried to do – then one other and final element needs to be added: the artist's perception. It's a very difficult element to discuss – being made up of many intangibles. But I'd like to look at my own work and try to indicate what I mean by development and show how I'd like to think my plays have developed.

As a playwright I'm mostly of the school which begins with experience rather than ideas. I'm not a writer who illustrates ideas, or explores ideas through invented characters and situations; rather I'm a writer whose experience drives me to organize that experience into a play or story because it seems to me to illuminate some aspect of human behaviour. There are some exceptions to this but it is generally true enough to be worth observing. So the plays I'd like to refer to are my first play, *The Kitchen*, and a play written twelve years later, *The Journalists*. Both are attempts to organize experience.

They both have other things in common as well: the form and the setting. Both have a large cast of about thirty who are on stage most of the time and both are set in a place of work: the kitchen of a huge restaurant; the offices of a large Sunday newspaper. They also have similar rhythms – *The Kitchen* begins with the chefs and waitresses slowly ambling into an empty space and preparing for a frenzied serving of lunch as the morning reaches its climax. *The Journalists* begins at the beginning of the week and slowly moves towards the frenzied activity on a Saturday when a national newspaper is being put to bed. In both we see people working and in both we glance in on their private lives and fears and attitudes. But here the similarities end.

There are two main differences. The first is that although both are based on experiences yet the experiencing was different. I actually worked for four years in kitchens – moving up from kitchen porter to pastry chef, whereas I never *worked* as a journalist, I'd only experienced journalism through reading newspapers in general and suffering personal interviews and reviews in particular, and had spent two months in the offices of the *Sunday Times* to obtain background material and knowledge of work methods.

The second difference is between the themes of the two plays. Whereas my experience of various kitchens produced the theme of the relationship of people to their work, my experience of journalism produced a much more complex theme: the relationship between the lilliputian mentality and a certain concept of democracy – a very difficult and dangerous thought.

The introduction to *The Journalists* ends:

The Kitchen is not about cooking, it's about people and their relationship to work. The Journalists is not about journalism, it's about the poisonous human need to cut better people down to our size, from which need we all suffer in varying degrees. To identify and isolate this need is important because it corrupts such necessary or serious human activities as government, love, revolution or journalism.

Swift wrote a novel which gave this cancerous need a name – lilliputianism. The lilliputian lover competes with his or her loved one instead of complementing him or her. The lilliputian journalist resents the interviewee's fame, influence or achievement rather than wishing to honour it or caution it or seriously question it. The lilliputian bureaucrat (involved in the same process but in reverse) seeks to maintain his own size by not acknowledging the *possibility of growth in those over whom he officiates; he doesn't <u>cut</u> down to size, he <u>keeps</u> down to size. The lilliputian revolutionary is more concerned to indulge resentments or pay off private scores than to arrive at real justice. Thus government, love, revolution or journalism are time and time again betrayed. It is this with which my play is concerned.*

It seems to me that I constantly return to experiences in my life which, as examples of this lilliputian mentality, have distressed and concerned me. The signs of this are there in that very first play, *The Kitchen*.

The Kitchen begins with a stage emptied of people. Only the kitchen itself looms. It is early morning. The night porter wakes. He puts a match to the gas ovens. He switches on the lights. A cook enters, prepares her 'station'. A kitchen porter appears, a waitress, another cook ... slowly the kitchen comes to life, preparation of food is mimed, different conversations flicker here and there across the stage, the first act ends in a frenzy of serving the lunch-time meal.

Next comes an interlude. Most of the chefs, porters and waitresses have gone to rest before returning to serve the evening meal. The central character, an exuberant, colourful but neurotic young German chef, is asking people what their hopes are, or what they dream about?

Each person says something. One hopes for money, another dreams of having many women, another wants to pursue his hobby, and so on. Last to speak is the pastrycook, Paul. And here is what Paul says:

PAUL … *Listen, Peter, I'll tell you something. I'm going to be honest with you. You don't mind if I'm honest? Right, I'm going to be honest with you. I don't like you. Now wait a minute – let me finish. I don't like you. I think you're a pig. You bully, you're jealous, you go mad with your work, you always quarrel. Alright! But now it's quiet, the ovens are low, the work has stopped for a little and now I'm getting to know you. I still think you're a pig, only now – not so much of a pig. So that's what I dream. I dream of a friend. You give me a rest, you give me silence, you take away this mad kitchen – so I make friends. So I think – maybe all the people I thought were pigs are not so much pigs.*

PETER *You think people are pigs, eh?*

PAUL *Listen, I'll tell you a story. Next door to me, next door where I live is a bus driver. Comes from Hoxton. He's my age, married, and got two kids. He says good morning to me, I ask him how he is,*

I give his children sweets. That's our relationship. Somehow he seems frightened to say too much, you know? God forbid I might ask him for something. So we make no demands on each other.

Then one day the busmen go on strike. He's out for five weeks. Every morning I say to him 'Keep going, mate, you'll win!' Every morning I give him words of encouragement, I say I understand his cause. I've got to get up earlier to get to work but I don't mind – we're neighbours – we're workers together – he's pleased.

Then one Sunday there's a peace march. I don't believe they do much good but I go, because in this world a man's got to show he can have his say. The next morning he comes up to me and he says, now listen to this, he says 'Did you go on that peace march yesterday?' So I says, yes, I did go on that peace march yesterday. So then he turns round to me and he says, 'You know what? A bomb should have been dropped on the lot of them! It's a pity', he says, 'that they had children with them 'cause a bomb should have been dropped on the lot!' And you know what was upsetting him? The march was holding up the traffic, the buses couldn't move so fast!

Now, I don't want him to say I'm right. I don't want him to agree with what I did – but what depresses me is that he didn't stop to think that this man helped me in my cause so maybe, only maybe, there's something in his cause – I'll talk about it. No! The buses were held up so drop a bomb, he says, on the lot! And you should have seen the hate in his eyes, as if I'd murdered his child. Like an animal he looked. And the horror is this – that there's a wall, a big wall between me and millions of people like him. And I think – where will it end? What do you do about it? And I look around me, at the kitchen, at the factories, at the enormous bloody buildings going up with all those offices and all those people in them, and I think – Christ! I think, Christ, Christ, Christ!

Now, that's the longest and only monologue there is in the play. For the rest it's all trivial exchange and the actions of a kitchen and the following-through of an ill-fated love affair between the main character and a married waitress who messes him around until, with everything else going wrong in the kitchen, he goes berserk and smashes the gas leads to the ovens, thus bringing the whole kitchen to a standstill.

Of course I like the play and think it's effective, and it seems to work as a powerful image all around the world (in fact it is the most performed of all my plays): the employer is bewildered by what happens and says, *'I give you plenty of work, good wages, you eat all you want – what more is there?'* The question is potent, potent but perhaps too simple. The action leading up to it is theatrically thrilling but there is no one around with a mind or imagination of any quality to shape the action at a more profound level or to react to lilliputianism at a more profound level.

With *The Journalists* there seemed to be more of an opportunity to do this. World-shattering and political lilliputian actions were going on off-stage and my central character was engaged in two very intellectually demanding activities: she was interviewing Conservative cabinet ministers for a special feature series under a 'science versus politics' heading; and she was also determined to expose a left-wing politician she thought was a phoney idealist. Twelve years on I was looking for lilliputians in much loftier places than the ranks of poor beleaguered bus drivers. I was looking at top-ranking, highly educated journalists.

The Journalists is set in the offices of a large Sunday newspaper which investigates in great depth government activity, foreign news, political issues; an important defender of freedom of expression. Imagine the stage divided into different spaces, perhaps at different levels. Each space is the office of a different department of the newspaper. Editor's Office, News Desk, Foreign Desk, Arts, Women, Business, Sport, etc. In each office are the different reporters. As in *The Kitchen* different conversations begin, different news items are introduced, dropped, picked up later, dropped again, picked up later, like a juggling act lots of balls are thrown in the air, linger there, are caught, thrown up again. The play operates on two time levels. Part One is Tuesday of week one. Part Two is Wednesday of week two. Part Three is Thursday of week three, and so on, ending on the last day, Saturday, when the newspaper is 'put to bed' – that is, finally printed and sent out for distribution. Dividing these days of many-peopled activity are the quieter interviews between the main character and the Conservative cabinet ministers. The next monologue is – to my mind – just as dramatically compelling as the pastry cook's but it reaches for an additional quality – intellect.

> *The office of Sir Roland Shawcross, the elegant and superior Minister for Social Services. A cassette recorder is close by. He is being interviewed by Mary Mortimer, a columnist in her mid-forties and renowned for her determined and apparently fearless energy.*

SHAWCROSS *And that, Miss Mortimer, is precisely what democracy is: a risky balancing act. The delicate arrangement of laws in a way that enables the state to conduct its affairs freely without impinging upon the reasonable freedom of the individual. Tilt it too much one way or the other and either side, state or individual, seizes up, unable to act to its fullest capacity.*

MARY *But surely, Minister, with respect, you must agree that the quality of democracy doesn't only depend on the balance of freedom which our laws create between the individual and society, does it?*

SHAWCROSS *By which you mean?*

MARY *By which I mean that you may give the letter to the law but ordinary men are forced, daily, to confront the depressing petty officials who interpret those laws.*

SHAWCROSS *Go on.*

MARY *I could go on endlessly, Sir Roland.*

SHAWCROSS *Go on endlessly. I don't see your question yet.*

MARY *Well, I'm rather intimidated about going on, you've said these things much better than ever I could.*

SHAWCROSS *Be brave.*

MARY *All right. Great wisdom and learning may be required to conceive statutes but who expects great wisdom and learning in officials? And the ordinary man meets them not you. He faces the policeman, the factory superintendent, the tax collector, the traffic warden – in fact the whole gamut of middle-men whose officious behaviour affects the temper and pleasure of everyday life.*

SHAWCROSS *And your question is?*

MARY *What concern do you have for that?*

SHAWCROSS *For the gap between the law maker and the law receiver?*

MARY *No, with respect, I'd put it another way. For the change in the quality of the law which takes place when mediocre men are left to interpret them.*

SHAWCROSS *That sounds like a very arrogant view of your fellow creatures, Miss Mortimer.*

MARY *Sir Roland, forgive me, I must say it, but that's evasive.*

Intercom buzzer rings

VOICE *Your car in fifteen minutes, Minister.*

SHAWCROSS *Thank you. (Pause.) Miss Mortimer, our first hour is nearly up. Tomorrow you're dining with us at home – it is tomorrow, I think? We can continue then. But for the moment I'd like to speak off the record. You've created a very unique repu-tation in journalism. Rightly and properly you're investigating the minds and personalities of men who shape policy. And you're doing it in depth, in our offices, our homes, and on social occasions. I'm surprised so many of us have agreed and perhaps it will prove a mistake. We'll see. But there are aspects of government which it's obviously foolish of* *us to discuss in public no matter how eager we are to be seen being open and frank. I'm not evasive but, to be blunt, some of my thoughts are so harsh they could be demoralising. Ah! you will say, that is the truthful part of the man I'm after. But I often wonder, how helpful is the truth? You're right, the ordinary man must face the numb and bureaucratic mind. Our best intentions are distorted by such petty minds. But that can't really be my area of concern, can it? I might then be forced to observe that the petty mind is a product of a petty education. Should I then go to complain to the Minister of Education. He might then say education is only part of the influence on a growing person – there's family environment to be considered. Should he then interfere in every man's home? No, no, no! Only God knows where wisdom comes from, you can't legislate for it. Government can only legislate for the common good; the individual good is, I'm afraid, what men must iron out among themselves. But I don't act on those thoughts. My attempts on legislation are not less excellent because I doubt the excellence of men to interpret them. So, which truth will you tell? That I aspire to perfection of the law? That I mistrust the middle men who must exercise*

*that law? Or will you combine the two? The first
is pompous, the second abusive, the third confusing.*

MARY *And you don't think people would respond to such
honesty?*

SHAWCROSS *No! Frankly I do not think most people
can cope with honesty.*

MARY *With respect, Minister, but that sounds like a very
arrogant view of your fellow creatures.*

SHAWCROSS *Ha!   (Pause.) We'll continue, we'll
continue. I must leave.*

Both go to the door which he holds open.

*And it's not necessary to keep saying 'with respect',
Miss Mortimer. Do you enjoy saying it? Funny
thing, but people enjoy saying things like 'your
honour' 'your Majesty' 'your highness' 'with respect'
…*

I think you'll see that what I'm trying to say is: part
of the nature of true development in a playwright – or
any artist – is to do with the greater complexity of experience they tackle and the more challenging thoughts

they offer for consideration. It is not to do with form, the form of my very first play engaged over thirty actors simulating work and all on stage at the same time – as complex and daring (or foolhardy) to handle as the play twelve years later.

But there is more to say. More challenging thoughts or a greater degree of intellect, may be one quality to look for, but there's another, even more important, which must be looked for if we are to find out whether our playwright has developed or not.

In case any of you were beginning to think I was saying simply that if a playwright becomes cleverer, ever wiser, it was sufficient ... I wasn't. I'm not. No, a more thoughtful artist *is* desirable if there's to be any development, but something in addition to thoughtfulness is needed: a sharper poetic sense. An artist whose *poetic* powers have grown is also a necessary prerequisite for one to be able to say of him or her, 'Ah! *There's* development.' But the question, 'What *is* the poetic sense, how do you define it, or identify it?' needs another half dozen lectures to explore – and I haven't written them!

Briefly, however. In constructing *The Journalists* I was very aware of two things: the rhythm which could be created by moving from department to department. It could not be arbitrary. The time spent in each place had to be the correct length, not too long, not too short.

And I was also aware of the special effect which could be created by juxtaposing one issue alongside another. That special effect, that juxtapositioning is what I call poetry in the theatre and it is indefinable. You can only place two passages alongside one another and trust it works for an audience, rather like editing a film and placing two images alongside one another. The correct juxtaposing of two objects in a room is called harmony, their relationship is pleasing. If you place two statements alongside each other so that, though unrelated, yet they intensify each other then that's what I think can be called poetic. I wish I could read a section of *The Journalists* in which such juxtapositioning takes place. You would see the poetic effect I *strove* for. But it is impossible with only one voice to read so many characters and make so many leaps from space to space.

The place of intellect in the theatre doesn't seem to me to rank very high these days. Both intellectual and emotional expectations drop as one waits for that curtain to rise. At best dramatists have learned the trick of making an audience *imagine* it's confronting a play of high intelligence – the illusion is strong but the actual intellectual demands less so.

In his book, *The Creative Experiment*, C.M. Bowra wrote: 'The effort of thought and the adventure and difficulty of finding the truth contribute to the poetical result by making it strong and more durable.' Thought helped creative writing to withstand the 'vagaries of taste'. Instinctive and spontaneous work had charm but lacked a 'reserve of power'. And then he phrased his thought in a way that just describes what my lecture has been trying to say as though he knew that one day I was going to write it. He said: 'It is a question of the degree to which the movements of the considering mind can contribute to the poetical effect by taking part in it ...' 'The considering mind contributing to the poetical effect.' The artist who can make those dance and come together has earned the description 'developed'.

A lecture delivered as part of a 'Writers' Day'
organised by PEN, May 1979

7. Notes to young playwrights

The difference between art as therapy
and art as experience

I T'S THE FIRST lesson to be learned.

The practice of any art form provides a degree of therapeutic benefit for the practitioner. But a work of art can't be only therapy. It must, in the end, be an extraordinary event on the stage (page, screen, canvas), it must result in a memorable experience for its audience.

If it's therapy for yourself that you're interested in then there exist groups where people get together to share their poetry, stories, plays as vehicles simply for getting something off their chest; places where you can tell part of your life-history that's been nagging you. Everyone has the need to 'express' themselves. It's a good thing that such groups exist; they provide an outlet for many who might otherwise choke on their frustrations. That's why children are encouraged to paint and write poetry at school. After 'expressing' themselves they feel released, unburdened, to a degree fulfilled. The paintings and poems may even possess a certain quality, a mood, a 'something'.

But art is not about 'expressing' oneself; it is about understanding, shaping, and being true to the material from which one has chosen to create a play. When it is written something of yourself may have been expressed – 'revealed' is perhaps a more accurate description – but to express or reveal should not be the reason for having written the play.

How do you know when one is therapy rather than art?

Because the impact of therapy is greater upon the person who has put it together than upon the recipient. Therapy is of more value to the person writing than the person reading or listening – to whom it can sometimes be tedious.

Experience, the raw material of both art and therapy, remains therapy when it is neither shaped nor infused with perceptions; when it has failed to metamorphose into that extraordinary theatrical experience that sends people away moved, disturbed, thoughtful, agitated, exhilarated.

The lethal seduction is to imagine that an incident or encounter that has amused or engaged us round the dinner table or in the street is axiomatically engaging or amusing on stage. Remember how often we've tried to recapture something for a friend that has happened to us and discovered our recapturing didn't match the experience? We couldn't quite convey the event as *we'd* experienced it.

How can our miserable failure be explained? In one of two ways perhaps: it wasn't worth trying to recreate – it was sufficient just to have experienced it; or we'd recreated it badly.

Which leads us to the next important note.

Distinguish between material that is the stuff of literature and material that is anecdotal.

THE ANECDOTE IS slight, merely good for conversation. Trying to transform it into drama is like trying to make a wooden doll stand in the square instead of a statue. Yes, something can *develop* from a dinner-table anecdote, but it's important to distinguish between what is heard and what it can become.

An important attribute of the writer is their ability to *select*. Life offers an enormous amount of material; add to it the riches of the imagination and what one confronts can be overwhelming.

By what they chose shall you know them could be inscribed at the head of any writing course.

Selection. Choice. Distinctions.

DISTINGUISH WHAT WILL be powerful, what *you* can make powerful on the stage. Distinguish between meanings, between intentions, between material that is anecdotal and material that resonates, carries meaning into other people's lives across time and frontiers.

Sort out what's to be used, what's to be dispensed with. Your craft demands that you select carefully, distinguish wisely or imaginatively, choose responsibly.

Example: I had a spinster aunt. She had to look after her mother, who died, then a sister, who died. She was hurt by the experience but seemed content to live alone and busy herself with visits to the family. There is nothing remarkable in such an experience. Sitting round a dinner table most guests could probably relate such a family story.

My aunt's history of lonely spinsterhood leaps ringing with resonance when it is revealed that she used to make crocheted bed-coverings for members of the family and, one day, having made hundreds of squares for a grand-nephew and sewn up all of them except thirty, she stopped. The last thirty remained unattached. She also stopped watering her plants, taking buses to visit us, washing herself. At one moment on a certain day her spirit wound down to a halt. Because in all of us there is a spirit waiting to give up she entered, on that day, into the stuff of drama.

Responsibility to the craft.

B E JEALOUS OF it as for a child from whom you want perfection. Perfection is an impossible state but that should not prevent the writer from aspiring to it! The writer has chosen his/her craft, no one else. It has not been chosen for them. And with such a choice comes responsibility, as with an adopted child. But it's not a one-way process. Respect your art and it will feed back with self-respect.

You must know everything your craft is capable of achieving. The stage can tell the story of an hour or of a hundred years. You can sail seas, go down a mine, fly a plane, ride a train. You can also, if you've found the right words, move audiences on a bare stage.

You must not be careless or indifferent. As serious about it as *you* are, so you will be taken seriously. If you merely 'toss' off any old thing then you too, in turn, will be tossed aside.

The artist as guardian of truths as they see them –

even unpleasant truths

even unpleasant truths about those you love or who are 'on your side'

even unpleasant truths which attract hostility from friends, colleagues, sisters, brothers

even uncomfortable truths which briefly place you in the 'enemy's camp'

THE ARTIST'S VOICE must be an individual's voice not the mouthpiece of groups or of a dogma. This is especially true in the age of 'political correctness' – a malfunctioning in human behaviour known in different ages by different labels such as: 'Puritanism', 'petty bourgeois', 'main street'.

Example: If you are a black, a Jewish, an Irish, a German writer and your experience of human relationships is that it sometimes breaks down for reasons rooted in inherited cultural characteristics – explore them! The same applies to gender. There are dreadful men who are dreadful in a way that is identifiably masculine, and there are dreadful women who are dreadful in a way that is identifiably feminine – tell it!

Which brings us to a fine paradox: we need to know there exists that one individual voice we can trust to say what he or she feels and thinks rather than mouth what is expected, what is most comfortable or opportune for them to mouth. When this happens, when the individual dares voice the unmentionable then it often turns out to be, unexpectedly, the voice of the many.

Artists must never, never be opportunists, but fiercely independent. Their talent is a unique gift given them for safekeeping, for cherishing, nurturing, for handing on in a dependable condition to the next generation of artists.

The individual vision is singular, the only hope for the future. The group may be needed for protection, preservation, co-operative physical endeavour, a sense of security, to give the individual a sense of belonging. But – no group should ever be given the right to stifle the individual voice or the group itself will be doomed.

Group decisions involve, inevitably, compromise. But too often the group finds it less trouble, less demanding to bless and support mediocrity, to be satisfied with the status quo and thus suffer atrophy. For this reason they need the voice of the independent artist. Such a voice is refreshing, often proving to be not the feared destroyer but the reviver of tradition, adding to it, even creating new ones.

To be an artist, then, requires patience to develop, enrich, hone your craft, and the courage to stand alone for what you've perceived and think about human beings and their condition.

An artist must not set out to intimidate, though that consequence may result from their work, nor should they allow themselves to be intimidated.

The craft of theatre involves –

a great deal more than people talking on a stage. It requires:

an understanding of the power of metaphor
an understanding of structure
a sense of rhythms of lines of speech
rhythms between lines
between sections
between scenes
between acts
a sense of place – settings
a sense of choreography – movement and actions
a clear understanding of characters:
their complexity
their contradictions
their perception of themselves
their perception of others
and you must be aware of how *you* perceive them.

Y OUR CRAFT REQUIRES an understanding of the distinction to be made between journalism and poetry, i.e. the tangible and the intangible.

Example: the making of a cup of tea on stage is journalism, tangible; the bursting into song, a leap in the air, a sudden smile – all for no apparent reason is (or could be) poetry, intangible; like the 'twang' of wire in Chekhov's *The Cherry Orchard*. Both are qualities needed in any work of art; but the greatest works of art have more poetry than journalism.

They will not love you forever –

neither critics nor those *in* the theatre. Therefore:
you must develop
never repeat yourself
keep inventing
keep your mind and imagination well-oiled by exposing yourself to all sorts of other artistic experiences.

T HE BEST ARTISTS usually have the effect of reviving our batteries, revealing to ourselves what more we've got within ourselves. Books, theatre, film, music – expose yourself to these and to all sorts of people and experiences, even the unpalatable. You must know those you want to attack better than they know themselves.

Listen not only to *what* people say but the *way* they say it.

Keep notes about those who interest you most. Record dialogue whose vigour strikes you.

Do not pursue what is absurd if what you've experienced does not call for the absurd. When it does call for it, use it! Nor engage irony when tenderness is called for, or lyricism if the mood requires harsh naturalism. Life comes too multifaceted to make a fetish of only one aspect of it. Reality is too complex to recreate it in a singular style, which then becomes a beloved 'personal signature'. I worry about writers who strait-jacket their material into personal mannerisms, which are mistaken, for their 'voice', or for their 'style'. Let your material dictate its own inherent style.

BUILD UP A BODY OF WORK IMPRESSIVE ENOUGH TO MAKE IT DIFFICULT FOR THEM TO DISMISS YOU.

New generations of writers are being born today who will inevitably challenge your place, and whom fickle critics and directors will want to champion because they're *new*. That's as it should be, but by that time *you* must have moved to another place; you must have created enough momentum to enable you to continue steadily and evade the demoralising feeling of being threatened.

Nothing, nothing, nothing stands still.

Nor must you!

1993, revived June 1995

8. The Playwright as Director

'No, I don't ever want to write plays. What? Put in a stage direction for a certain kind of yellow hat to be worn, one that's absolutely representative of the character's personality and you can be sure they'll get the wrong bloody colour if they bother to get a hat at all because the actress is allergic to things on her head or something! Give me prose every time where the reader reads exactly what I've written whether I'm making mistakes or not ... at least they're my mistakes.'

Margaret Drabble, novelist

IT IS NOT questioned that a composer can conduct his own music or a film director direct his own film; it is inconceivable, though physically possible I suppose, that someone else should paint the painter's canvas; the novelist and poet, have complete control of their material – except in translation, of course.

The arguments against the playwright directing his or her own play seem to go like this: (1) the dramatist cannot be objective about his work. The play as written has one dimension but for staging it requires the kind of objectivity that will permit a new dimension to be added – which can best be achieved by a director: the author imagines all his words are sacrosanct, and besides, doesn't always understand his own play. (2) The playwright only *writes* the play. He has no appreciation of the technical problems involved in mounting it: what works on the desk is one thing, the stage is another. (3) Actors are inhibited in front of the writer and cannot experiment or play around with the roles in different ways. Handling the actor, understanding his problems, demands a different temperament from the one normally found in a writer. The writer may know what he wants but he doesn't know how the actor must reach it. We're instinctive, the writer is intellectual.

Having attended the rehearsals of all ten of my plays on stage, four again on TV, one again in the film studio, and having directed five of them myself – one (unhappily) in England, and four abroad – I'm in a position to comment on these objections which are, except for one, most curious.

One: objectivity is presumably the ability to detach oneself – from the love, concern, fears, emotion and intellect invested in the play – in order to be critical about it. This, it is said, the writer cannot do. The objection betrays no understanding of the creative process, a process in which many drafts of a work may be written, *each draft being the result of the writer's objectivity about the previous one*! Every new draft cuts, tightens, deepens, rearranges; a critical faculty is constantly in use. Why should that critical faculty, that objectivity, cease to function the moment the play enters rehearsal – the one period when the writer can most clearly see and be shown the play's faults? The objection has no logic.

A new dimension, it is true, can be brought to the production of a play by a director. But are all *new* dimensions inevitably *good* dimensions? There does exist the danger of an *incorrect* dimension. Perhaps the phrase 'new dimension' belongs more to the *often* performed play which is so familiar to theatregoers that a 'new dimension' can bring fresh light on the play's meaning, whereas a *new* play on its first exposure should be allowed to emerge with the *author's* concept of its dimensions – warts and all!

Or let's ask this question: if the world premiere of a new play were given simultaneous productions in six of the best reps in the country would all six stagings communicate the *same* new dimensions? Obviously not. Therefore wouldn't the author's interpretation be at least as interesting as those other six? Or is it suggested that, however mediocre, the six productions would all be better than the author's because there is some magic about an 'outsider's' view?

And then, what precisely can this 'new dimension' of the outsider's be? The play – hopefully – is already one man's new dimension of his experience. Can it be that a director is adding a new dimension to the new dimension? There could be dangers in that. The danger of censorship: the added dimension to the new dimension blocks out the new dimension! (I've deliberately allowed the absurdity to blossom.) Or the danger of confusion of vision: 'I too have a point of view, you know!' Or of trivializing: 'You must be more comprehensible.' Or of defusing: 'To be more acceptable.'

But these dangers are easy to counter. Much more insidious are the suggestions for change in text, characterization, emphasis or rhythm which seem perfectly sensible but which are wrong *for reasons the author has forgotten*! Plays, though they appear to be simply an effort to put words into the mouths of recognizable characters who are involved in an engaging plot or set of relationships, are in fact very complex structures.

An author sometimes spends hours balancing six sentences in a monologue to ensure: (1) they belong to the character uttering them; (2) they have intellectual or emotional dynamic that is both compelling and valid; (3) they have rhythm; (4) they appear at the right and inevitable point in the scene, and so on. Sometimes he achieves all this instinctively and without effort, but usually the reasons or instincts he's brought to bear in the achievement are, odd though it may sound, often forgotten. It is very easy, then, for a director to deflect an author from his intentions, especially in the heat of rehearsals when 'the actors mustn't be disturbed now' or 'this is the wrong psychological moment to bring it up' (and then it becomes too late to bring it up!) or 'they're producing something else, isn't it magnificent?' or 'they're working so hard for you now, you can't tell them they're wrong, go away.'

The need, I think, is not for a 'new dimension' but for something much simpler and more necessary: an opinion. I owe many changes in my plays to the opinions of friends, but it's not unreasonable that a certain moment is reached – by most playwrights – when they've used up the present supply of 'objectivity' and require recharging by an opinion authoritatively founded in theatrical experience – a director's, an actor's, a set designer's. For this reason I also owe certain changes in my plays to John Dexter (who directed my first five plays). But, and here is the interesting point, though changes were made to *The Old Ones* under Dexter's direction in London, yet other changes were made to the play under my own direction in Munich. The conclusion could be that it is the *possibility* for change which encourages change, not the person. Give an author the chance to direct his own play and he will change as crisply and perceptively as any director.

Two: 'The desk is one thing, the stage another.' I've tried hard to consider that this objection might have some justification. But can it really be true for the serious, professional writer? On the contrary, alone at the desk one has all the time in the world to persuade oneself that *everything* one does is wrong.

Most people at work in the theatre would agree that it is neither possible nor desirable to write in the stage directions for every shift of limb, flick of eye or intonation of voice, but I'm very conscious of the physical relationships of characters to one another, of particular actions while speaking, of the emotive effect of colours and textures, the visual impact of structures, the choreography of movement, the speed of delivery. All these are elements woven into the fabric of the play. Far from being indifferent to complex theatrical possibilities many writers are fearful that their inventiveness and craftsmanship will be missed or ignored by conservative actors and directors in a hurry.

It is possible to have made impossible demands of the theatre, rehearsals show one what those are; but the greater danger is for the playwright's innovations to be crippled. The best playwrights make not impossible but unfamiliar demands upon the theatre, they stretch the theatre's preconceived limitations. If the desk *is* one thing and the stage another then all the more reason for a playwright to come closer to his material.

Three: the actor/director relationship touches upon what is central to all productions. Two preliminary points: actor/writer relationships have a long history, longer than actor/director; and if they fail it may have to do only with a clash of personalities and not because it is a bookish old writer failing to understand the delicate, vulnerable actor – the evidence for which lies in the ruins of many actor/director relationships.

'We're instinctive, the writer is intellectual.' Sometimes yes, sometimes no, sometimes both. But in any case what of the many directors who come from the intellectual disciplines of a university? And how to describe those writers who have come from the anarchy of a varied work existence? Such writers could say, "We're experienced in real life, the actor is cloistered.'

As for the actor being inhibited before the author – I've rarely experienced it, except in the early days of rehearsal when actors are just as likely to be inhibited before each other.

Very often it's the actor who wants to deliver emotional lines emotionally and I've found myself having to force him to fight against my text. As director I've always patiently encouraged actors to twist texts inside out, act against them, try saying tragic lines with humour, lyrical ones vulgarly. Far from inhibiting or tensing an actor I've found my presence relieved him because he felt the one person who could give him an answer to his questions was right there.

But that a difference exists in temperament between actor and writer is true, and could fairly be offered as a reason why the playwright should not direct his own play. It is worth looking at. The craft of the actor is a complex one, and an essay as brief and tentative as this would not presume to be exhaustive about it; but to further this defence of the playwright as director here is an observation which perhaps has not been sufficiently considered before.

Paradoxically, basic to an actor's fear is his vulnerability to the accusation of 'acting'. He's vividly aware that society normally uses the name of his profession as the name of an abuse: 'Oh, ignore him, he's just acting'. 'Just acting' is the actor's *raison d'être,* his means of livelihood. He asks an audience to forget that acting is to pretend to be what and who you are not – which is rightly frowned upon in everyday encounters. What is despised in a person *off*-stage the actor asks us to praise *on*-stage. In the audacity of this request lies his terror. This is why he fights; sometimes his fellow actors, sometimes the director, sometimes the set designer, costumier, author, audience; sometimes all of them, sometimes the wrong ones. Any one of them might be leading him to make a fool of himself. The terror is absolutely understandable. No profession can be so racking as that where a person exposes himself to the ridicule of disbelief and the attendant ignominy of dismissal, the humiliation of being 'seen through'.

Who succeeds? Most actors will agree – very few. They are constantly 'seeing through' each other. But those who do break through the brittle and sour barrier of scepticism perform a miracle. To experience them is to witness men and women possessed. We all kneel before them. It happens rarely, however.

What is it the actor must do? Personally I believe the skill rests not in him being able to 'pretend' better than the next, but in *not caring* that he is pretending. The bad actor is usually one so worried to be caught pretending that he plays to be loved, or he plays what will easily amuse – and so be forgiven for pretending. One can sense his uneasiness, he communicates it to us through self-consciousness. Either he walks clumsily or he puts on 'a voice': 'see, I know I'm pretending really, so don't hurt me.' Or it produces that school of acting where the actor's style is one of pretending not to pretend; yet even that approach degenerated into cosy mannerisms, despite some fine performances by Brando. But the great actor is – or appears to be – so intensely indifferent to the existence of the audience that, again the paradox, only through such total indifference does the audience feel he is really performing for them.

Now, the responsibility for guiding an actor and helping him shape the performance in which he will not make a fool of himself, is an awesome one. In assuming directorship the author divides his loyalties between a responsibility to his play and a responsibility to his actors. Sometimes they are in conflict because, too late to change, it is discovered that an actor does not have the correct set of registers and ranges to fulfil the part for which he's been cast. It's not a question of an inferior range, simply a *different* one. That scene will now never reach its intended mood, this speech will now never ring in its true pitch, that argument will now never be fully understood, that 'moment of truth' will now never be revealed in all its terror. But the play and the actor will be irretrievably damaged if he is forced to do what he is not equipped to do and the function of the writer/director at that moment is to ignore the demands of the play and look for an *equivalent* approach from out of the resources the actor *does* possess.

It is not always easy. But then what is? What talent doesn't mature through experience or involve exposure to mistakes? A craft must be learnt. And even so, directors who've had all the experience in the world have suffered nervous breakdowns.

My argument is this: there is no mystique inherent in the craft of directing, the craft can be learnt. The learning may not make a great director but *it can be learnt*. And if the author has the wish, the inclination, the patience, he, like the director, can command the craft through experience. More, *if* it can be learnt then the combination of the two talents in the one man is formidable and, potentially, thrilling.

Postscript: Of oblique but important relevance to the question of the playwright's estrangement from his work, is the overall phenomenon of the creative artist's isolation by all those who have to interpret, present, represent and comment upon his work. Three encounters have brought this home to me in the last months.

One of our finest novelists recently returned from a lecture tour of the United States where she was feted by her publisher in New York. 'You have no idea', she said, 'of the extraordinary sense of redundancy one feels among all these publishers, editors, agents, journalists. As though they'd been gathered together to meet each other rather than oneself.'

It was not a paranoiac complaint about rejection but an observation concerning the artist's alienation, measurements of regard. Impressed on her was a sense that her work was a commodity to be weighed, evaluated, speculated upon rather than esteemed for its literary merit or warmed to for its powers of perception. It was assumed she'd have no further interest in her 'commodity' nor understand the process which 'of necessity' had to take it over.

Then came the report from a friend, a young professor of literature, who'd just returned from an international conference organized by one of the new universities; the conference had themes to discuss such as 'Relation between ideology and literature'; 'The need for historicism'; 'The study of literature as an aspect of the study of "operations of cultural communications"'; 'The extrinsic and intrinsic approaches to the sociology of literature with particular reference to Dickens's *Oliver Twist*'. She, the young professor, lamented how not only was the conference arid because no living artist was present but, worse, his presence would have been superfluous. In fact, she observed wryly, a real artist might have embarrassingly gotten in the way! All that was important were theories about criticism, and responses to those theories, and responses to those responses.

The third encounter was with a young painter whose gallery takes 50 per cent of his earnings from sales (most galleries take 33.3 per cent which is outrageous enough). Not only that, but no regular account was rendered to him of *what* was sold, he had no way of checking for *how much* a painting was sold, he was not informed *who* bought the paintings (for fear he'd go to them privately to sell his work, thus by-passing the gallery), and occasionally paintings were 'lost'. The attitude of the entrepreneurs reduced him to feeling like an intruder and believing that favours were being done for him.

Time and again one meets with artists who are made to feel intruders in their own profession. Only once did I hear a reassuring story: a composer friend, Wilfred Josephs, whose Requiem had won a prize from La Scala and the City of Milan, told me how, when he'd gratefully thanked the conductor, Giulini, for accepting to conduct the work around the world, he, Giulini, replied in this vein: 'You shouldn't thank me. It is for me to thank you. I'm only the conductor.'

Many artists, of course, choose to stay outside, to toss their works into the melee and let come what may. For example, playwrights and novelists find their work, sometimes cheaply bought by the film industry, slaughtered out of all recognition by producers whose priorities are other than artistic, or by directors who feel their interpretations to be of greater significance than the original. I've witnessed foreign productions of my plays in which poetry, meaning and structure were sacrificed in order to squeeze the play into the strait-jacket of a director's concept.

In the years between writing, painting or composing his next work, in those years of silence when it is so easy for the artist to feel forgotten, the men in the middle are constantly busy handling other artists' work, fuelled into activity by their many creative talents, working when *apparently* the artist is not. Disproportionate importance is garnered because they are always kept engaged; the critic's efforts, for instance, appear every day or every weekend – such a continual presence illogically demands a greater degree of serious attention than the artist whose work appears every one, two, perhaps three years. The conductor conducts so often that it must almost seem as though *he* has composed the music. Everyone has heard of Andre Previn, rather fewer have heard of Wilfred Josephs.

It is, of course, very difficult for those in the professions which stand between the creative artist and the public *not* to feel disproportionately important. The novelist who confronts a publisher and awaits judgment is not an artist standing before just any man, he's confronting a man through whom *many* novelists have passed. The publisher may not be a creative writer himself but behind him, intimidatingly, are the names of all the other writers he's published. His importance is composed of the literary achievements of other men who come together in him and thus make the poor writer feel he's nothing compared to them. The young painter doesn't feel he is intruding on the time of merely the gallery owner, but of the gallery owner who has hung such great names as... The young dramatist who's insisting his play be performed as *he* conceives it isn't arguing with directors and actors, he's arguing with directors and actors who have interpreted (and reflect) the glory of the plays of such great dramatists as...

This optical illusion, this sleight of hand can be paralleled in *all* the arts, and it is the final paradox: the artist is isolated by the combined talents of his colleagues which, together, must loom weightily when assembled in the one man who has published, acted or sold them all – which 'one man' is usually not reluctant to let that weight be felt.

It is not healthy. The creative artist is easily demoralized. In the medium of the drama, whether stage, radio, TV or film, the writer is subjected to four different kinds of censorship, before his work reaches a public: the producer, the director, the actor, the critic.

He has to fight hard to ensure that his own voice emerges through all those filters. Even when it does there is the final hazard of the 'aftermath commentator'.

I'm desperately thankful to have passed most of these hurdles and been fortunate enough to have slowly commanded the right (and the technique) to control my own work. I would like to see young dramatists encouraged and trained in the craft. If nothing else it will enrich their theatrical imaginations.

February 1974

9. Individual Opinions Magnified out of Proportion by Print – a review of a collection of James Fenton's theatre reviews, 'You Were Marvellous.'

JAMES FENTON'S NATURE doesn't appear to be vindictive, though wiser playwrights would run miles from such a risk as I now take. I declare my interest: two of my plays have been the subject of his comments. Those for *Caritas* I'd heard were not favourable and did not read. The practice of the craft is pain enough without subjecting oneself to the cruel ephemerality of a reviewer's opinion. When I've written this I'll read it and add a postscript. Those for *Annie Wobbler,* my latest play, were generous.

Criticism is crucial to democracy. So crucial it must be checked and weighed and constantly be open to counter-criticism. Assembling one's critical opinions after only four years may seem like immodest haste to claim posterity's attention, but four years *is* four years. The problem of evaluating theatre is that no one dares make, or quite knows, the distinction between the lovely lady, showbiz, and the embarrassing slut, art. Criteria become jumbled. 'You were marvellous' is a showbiz expression. It does not reflect Mr Fenton's serious criteria. Where are we?

The cosy argument is that artists hate criticism. Not true. We are relentlessly self-critical, and most of us have at least one acerbic friend whose criticism is invaluable. Criticism from colleagues involved in theatre is constant up to and beyond first nights. The Penguin editions of my plays are full of changes.

Newspaper reviews, on the other hand, render the artist victim of a dangerous deception for which I know no remedy. It can only be identified. The nature of the deception is this: reviews are merely individual opinions whose importance is magnified out of proportion by print, which has magic properties and carries awesome authority. Like a teacher's report. Teachers must always be right, they've been appointed. The child can only ever be wrong.

Fenton in his postscript honestly concedes the possibility of being, and claims the right to be, wrong. It's disarming. But jejune. 'We must be true to our anger, true to our enthusiasms, true to our excitement, true to our boredom,' he insists. It can only ever be a half-truth. Behind his anger, his enthusiasm, his etc., etc. is the *Sunday Times*. We are not pitted only against him but against an institution. Reviewers like to delude themselves they have a public who trusts them. But did anyone change papers because Fenton took over from Levin?

There's more to the deception. Aware of it or not, the public regards artistic activity as presumptuous. Unfavourable reviews play to their gallery. Artists acclaimed by time are safer. Living ones work in a continual state of original sin from which only a good review can redeem them. They're a kind of criminal; the public must be protected. The reviewer is St George, print his sword! The reader, who thrills to a good thrashing, is on his side before he begins.

If artists feel a depressing sense of injustice confronted by an adverse review, it's not because they've been criticized but because they've been criticized humiliatingly in public by an overwhelming institution whose sleight of hand appears to deal omnipotently in 'the truth', and against which the artist has no appeal.

A story illustrates my point. *Caritas* had just opened. At a friend's house I met an elderly, cultured woman I'd met before. We usually discussed theatre and she'd confide how much she admired my work. I didn't need to ask had she seen my new play, I *told* her she hadn't. 'It was because of Fenton's bad review, wasn't it?' I added. She apologetically confessed I was right. 'But why', I asked her in despair, 'why did you trust him rather than me?' I reminded her how often she'd told me she'd admired my work. 'Why didn't you give me the benefit of the doubt after twenty-five years of writing?' She mumbled something about 'he wrote in such a way that I felt it wasn't for me'. She could have had no idea of the helpless, dispirited feeling with which she left me.

Two problems attend the reading of an entire collection of theatre reviews in one go. First, you need to have seen the productions to measure the opinions offered. Criticism of a play frequently bears little relationship to the experience of it. Second, to have the critical note ringing in your head without the pauses of living, loving and laughing is a kind of torture, like the water-drip. Reading only one a week, it's possible to recognize Mr Fenton as a normal, intelligent human being with opinions like other normal, intelligent human beings, sometimes persuasive, witty, well written, other times not. He's informed, seems to take more trouble than duty calls for, has winning breathless enthusiasms and pure hatreds like other normal, intelligent human beings.

And this is why we despair. It *is* just another opinion; as intelligent or flawed as those of countless acquaintances. The sense of injustice comes from knowing one is condemned not on merit but by the accident of A's appointment to the job rather than B's.

In my opinion Fenton missed the intention of *Amadeus* which, as a self-confession of mediocrity and a hymn of praise to genius, makes it a far more interesting and moving work then he perceived. (And I write as someone who doesn't normally respond to Shaffer's kind of theatre.) He was right to applaud *Duet For One,* and to come away depressed from *Cats;* but he was uninteresting about Barton's distressing *Merchant of Venice,* and did not achieve in his review of *The Greeks* what his introduction claims was his intention; a record of the production's details. I disagree with this opinion, agree with the other. So what?

Few who work in the theatre rate a reviewer's opinions. They care only to survive the new round of unsubstantiated, shorthand comment rushed and subbed and laced with human fallibility. When asked whether they are pleased with good reviews they reply, 'Relieved, rather'. They've lived with a production at such proximity that they know it for its *real* strengths and weaknesses. Reviewers confuse sentiment for sentimentality, and declare something doesn't work when they mean they don't share its intellectual or moral assumptions. Or don't understand them! They miss subtleties of structure, speech rhythms, textural patterns, ironies, echoes, links, the way actors and directors can either betray a text's intentions or, through cunning directoral manipulation, give text a substance it doesn't possess. Theatre people can damn and praise their own work far more accurately.

Mr Fenton declares: Critics unite! In order to begin work we need the right to be wrong, the right to be unfair, the right to be over-enthusiastic. But at whose expense? And what curious reasoning claims 'the right to be unfair'? It rings bravely but I hear the tiniest crackle of sententiousness. A year to write a play, a year before it's produced, then those unassailable reviews claiming the right to be unfair. Two years of work wiped out, two years more to wait. Such considerations cannot be dismissed as 'tough luck-that's showbiz.' Livelihoods, cracked confidence, pain are involved. Each time a new, young critic takes over we brace ourselves fearing he is going to flex his muscles on us, beat a drum calling the crowds' attention – 'Over here! over here!' Mr Fenton must be aware he's doing more than simply exercising his right to be wrong when he writes of Shaffer: 'Mozart is depicted in an offensive and banal way because he is seen through the eyes of a very, very bad dramatist indeed – perhaps the worst serious English dramatist since John Drinkwater.' Could he cross his heart and deny that one tiny part of his ego rubbed its hands together, smacked its lips and murmured: 'That'll make 'em sit up'?

Postscript. I've read Mr Fenton's review of *Caritas*. It is a very illuminating case history of misreading. I have a theory that if you tell people what they're reading, *that* is what they'll read. Tell them here is a play by Wesker and they'll find what they *imagine* is to be expected of Wesker. I recently wrote a bawdy comedy, which was sent to managements as the work of a Cambridge professor of philosophy. Responses reflected what they'd been told. Similarly Mr Fenton seems to have an image of me as a certain kind of writer.

Caritas is about an anchoress who asks to be immured, hoping for a pure life of divine revelation. She finds she has no vocation for such a life, begs release, is denied it and goes mad. '*Caritas* is extremely badly written,' says Mr Fenton. I say it is extremely well written. More, in view of the misery of young people inextricably attached to fanatical notions, which have imprisoned them, I think *Caritas* as a metaphor for self-delusion is, also, an important play. Who is to be believed? After a quarter of a century writing plays (directing and viewing them too) it is just possible I knew at least as much about it as Mr Fenton. How could readers decide? His review acted as a kind of censor to the play. Criticism of critics reads sourly. Self-defence involves immodest assertions. Catch **22.**

Asking 'What was Mr Wesker after?' Fenton, unwaveringly confident – and why shouldn't he be, there was no one to challenge him – replies: 'The answer is only too clear from the text ... an image of repression.' He *expected* me to be writing about repression and that's what he saw. In truth the text is only too clearly about a girl who *asks* to be immured, not who *is forced* into it. The image is of self-imprisonment. Setting it against the background of the Peasants' Revolt I was choosing not another 'image of repression' but, again as the text clearly states, another image of self-destruction. Both the anchoress and the peasants sought worthy ends, both betrayed those ends through excess, dogma, fanaticism.

Mr Fenton, still blinded by his preconceptions, suggested I had changed the setting from Surrey to Norfolk in search of '*grittiness*'. Readers cannot be expected to know my connections with Norfolk through marriage (*Roots, The Wedding Feast);* a responsible theatre critic on the other hand should. I knew one dialect, not the other. *'He has obviously done very little research.'* Why does Mr Fenton assume so? He doesn't know me. He didn't ask. In fact I researched the background to *Caritas* in great detail, as my many notebooks testify. All art is selection. He means he doesn't respond to what I decided to put in and leave out. He should say so. Insults diminish the value of his opinions, especially since he seems merely to have read the dust-jacket of the Penguin *Julian of Norwich*. This is not only a defence of my play; such a case history enables us to evaluate Mr Fenton's reliability as a reviewer. Other playwrights could no doubt argue similar cases.

Dear Mr Fenton, I concede your right to be wrong (though not unfair, come, come, sir!), even to be paid for it. But be aware others pay a hidden price for your luxury. The life of a play is postponed, a bank overdraft grows, time is wasted recovering. *Caritas* is one of my most original plays. Years must pass before it can be re-evaluated. Many of us work hard, seriously, responsibly. We take risks, we treat our audiences intelligently, prod their laughter at rich rather than facile levels. These reviews, whatever the lapses, reveal a responsible intelligence that we need to encourage us to continue taking risks. Don't go into competition with us or demean yourself with pyrotechnic insults. And remember, *we* have to continue working after *you* have become bored with our art (as your photograph suggests you prematurely are) and have moved on to other interests.

25 August 1983

On 30 August Bernard Levin devoted his weekly column to commenting on the above article in the *Listener.* He began by generously describing the piece as 'an excellent article written with elegance and passion ... formidable, fair and logically argued ...' He had *'never seen it better done'*. He then proceeded to summarize and criticize. He was careless, misquoted, exaggerated my position, observed *'this argument can never end'* and concluded with T. C. Worsley *'that theatre and critic could never be lasting friends, because they work from different premises.'* His piece was entitled 'Darlings, you're not quite as wonderful as you think'.

I wrote a reply, which *The Times* declined to print. It was entitled 'But you, Bernard, are as wonderful as you think'.

Meanwhile, back at *The Times Literary Supplement* (2 September 1983), my fellow playwright Simon Gray had also written an article inspired by James Fenton's book of reviews. Fenton was given space in the *Sunday Times* (4 September 1983) to respond to us both. I was allowed to enter the letter columns with a reply to that. Richard Boston rounded it all up in the *Guardian* (24 September 1983).

10. On The Nature of Theatre Dialogue

B EFORE I BEGIN let me remind you that I speak as a practitioner who is attempting to understand what he has done rather than as a theoretician who is postulating the way it *should* be done. And, even when I think I've understood what I've done, I do not conclude with theories. Theory is what excites the academic mind. Personally I'm a theory-sceptic – I fear theory becoming a prescription for the way things *must* be done. Theory breeds rules that destroy the innovative imagination; it becomes a barrier against new discoveries.

The best that can be said about theory is that after creation it can explain what the artist has achieved, what new frontiers the artist has opened; or theory can produce arguments for what should *not* be done. And that is useful, but it should be understood for what it is. I suspect that a great work of art produces theory about itself and perhaps a few other works, but not about *all* art.

Two observations:

the first – no dialogue can ever correspond to reality;

the second – the texture of the dialogue, like the form of the play itself, is dictated by the material. I'll explain this as we go along.

I make that first observation as often as I can because I consider it of primary importance: no dialogue can ever correspond to reality. More – no art can ever correspond to reality either. There can be no such thing as realistic art. The notion of realistic art is a contradiction in terms. Even in our daily lives we cannot experience total reality, since a moment of reality is made up of much more than we are able to experience or comprehend.

This moment of reality, for example; one that is taking place now cannot be known by anyone in this room because none of you can see the person behind you or the face of the person in front of you or know what anyone is thinking. This moment of reality also consists of what is happening outside this room. We don't know what that is. Nor do we know what's happening outside this building, this town, this state, this country, this continent, this globe. So, because we are unable to experience total reality we are therefore unable to recreate it in art. But – and this is a very important difference – all art *deals* with reality, *handles* reality, even though it's only a limited reality. And sometimes art deals absurdly with what is naturalistic in reality, sometimes art deals naturalistically with what is absurd in reality. You can permutate at length but the fact would remain: art cannot *be* reality, it can only *deal* with reality because reality can be only partly known and partly comprehended.

The next question is: what does 'dealing with' involve? Whatever we're doing – whether, like Ionescu, we're dealing with naturalistic behaviour in an absurd form, or, like Chekhov, with absurd behaviour in a naturalistic form – what is the process? What exactly is happening when we're 'dealing with'?

The answer invokes the classic formulation with which you are familiar: all art is selection. When we're 'dealing with' reality we are *selecting* from it. And we are selecting *out of necessity;* we can't help ourselves, and for these two reasons: one, as I've already tried to explain, because artists can know only a *part* of reality; and two, because it is in the nature of any one work of art that it cannot physically handle every second, every sigh, every nuance. The limitations of what we can possibly know and understand – this is one force at work in selection; the limitation of any art form itself is the second force at work in selection. Limited comprehension and the limitation of an art's form – these two limitations control us as artists.

There is a third element engaged while selecting from reality – and it is only here that we have a degree of choice and control. I'm not sure what word to use to describe what governs that choice. Our taste? Our values? Our poetic sensibility? All three? Let's call this third element 'poetic sensibility'. The third element that artists engage when selecting from their experience of reality is their poetic sensibility.

And here I repeat my first argument: for these very same reasons – the limitations of form and the limitations of what can be known – *stage dialogue* can never be realistic. It must also be selected.

The next two questions are: why is one assembly of dialogue selected by the writer rather than another? And how is its form arrived at? And here we come to a kind of mystery.

I am not a semanticist and have read little on the subject. What I've tried to read I've found to be mostly incomprehensible. But I was first made aware that the subject existed at all by an Israeli friend many years ago. He said to me, 'We have resolved everything except one question.' I won't repeat that question yet. Instead here's a short extract from a play I wrote called *Annie Wobbler,* part of a cycle of plays for one woman.

The actress has to play three different characters: an old tramp of 60, a young student of 25, and a middle-aged novelist whose fourth novel is a huge success. This last character is about to be interviewed by three journalists. She is weary from all the interviews she's had to confront, and by now she knows the kind of questions she will be asked. She is rehearsing her answers and has decided to present two different news-worthy 'personae' for which she thinks the journalists are looking, which will make good copy.

The first is the bewildered, modest, humble 'persona', the kind of writer who claims that her work has nothing to do with her – she is merely the medium through which the muse works. The second is the arrogant writer pretending she writes only for fame, money, and power. But the third persona she offers is the kind of writer she really is – one terrified and full of doubts about the quality of her talent.

Her name is Annabella. She is answering the question, "Can you say what drives you to write?" She searches painfully for the inexplicable. She thinks it began with wanting to write poetry, which leads her to ask the question:

> *Why is it that a certain selection of words arranged in a certain way explode in you and yet, change one word, one syllable and there's not even a damp spark?*

I keep getting this urge, you see, to write poetry. It's a very strong urge and I become filled with a special kind of ... kind of ... how can it be described? An incorporeal expectation. A bit like being on heat. And out it comes, this poetry, this selection of words and images I <u>think</u> is poetry. And it's shit. And a pain. Such a pain. You've no idea the pain it is to begin with this heat, this fever, this sense that an astonishing assembly is about to take place and all that assembles is shit? Listen:

> *'Well, world, you have kept faith with me,*
>   *Kept faith with me.'*

Miraculous aren't they? Thomas Hardy. Simple, but – a magic assembly.

> *'Well, world, you have kept faith with me,*
>   *Kept faith with me.'*

Now-

> *'World world, you have kept faith with me ...'*

Not quite the same is it?

> *'Well world, you've kept your faith*
> *Kept your faith.'*

Not really.

> *'Well, world, with me your faith was kept*
> *Your faith was kept.'*

I don't think so.

> *'Well, world, you have kept faith with me,*
> *Kept faith with me;*
> *Upon the whole you have proved to be*
> *Much as you said you were.'*

[Achingly] To be a poet ...

And that was the Israeli semanticist's question: we have solved everything except the question of what makes one sentence a line of poetry and what makes another sentence dull, lifeless. I don't know if the semanticists have since answered the question, but the point I want to make is that one element of great dialogue is inexplicable: its poetic power.

I'm not talking about a poetic line from the great verse dramatists – that is *pure* poetry. I'm talking about the poetic power of a line that, in addition to its poetic power, is immediately acceptable as everyday speech, and yet is not exactly everyday speech. Where does its power come from? Perhaps it is only possible to describe *where* it comes from but not explain *why it should be so.*

Let's try to break down the 'where'. The power of an assembly of words for the stage, which we call dialogue, comes from five needs:

the need to belong to character;

the need to inform;

the need to communicate meaning;

the need to have rhythm – internal rhythm and a rhythm relating to a previous and a subsequent line;

and finally the need for sound.

Characterisation, information, meaning, rhythm, and sound.

HERE ARE A few lines from the opening of the second play I ever wrote though it was the first to be performed – *Chicken Soup With Barley*, the first of a trilogy of plays which came to be known as *The Wesker Trilogy*. It is often imagined that because *Chicken Soup* deals with political disillusionment that therefore it is about ideas and not about people. I have never written about ideas; rather I've written about people who are animated by ideas. And so *Chicken Soup* is primarily about a family whose disintegration as a family parallels the disintegration of their political beliefs.

Chicken Soup opens with anti-fascist demonstrations in the East End of London in 1936. A communist couple, Jewish, are preparing themselves to take part. These are the first lines in the play:

SARAH *[From the kitchen]* You took the children to Lottie's?

HARRY *[Taking up book to read]* I took them.

SARAH *They didn't mind?*

HARRY *No, they didn't mind.*

SARAH *Is Hymie coming?*

HARRY *I don't know.*

SARAH *[To herself]* Nothing he knows! *[To HARRY]* You didn't ask him? He didn't say? He knows about the demonstration, doesn't he?

HARRY *I don't know whether he knows or he doesn't know. I didn't discuss it with him – I took the kids, that's all. Hey, Sarah, you should read Upton Sinclair's book about the meat-canning industry – it's an eye-opener ...*

SARAH *Books! Nothing else interests him, only books. Did you see anything outside? What's happening?*

Consider the sounds, and the rhythms – they belong to Jewish speech rhythms. Consider character, the mother's character, she who cares. Consider the father's character, who cares but cares less. Consider their relationship – she chastising, he protesting, evading; they are always on the edge of a quarrel. Consider how the rhythms of each line hangs on the curve of the other. And all this is contained in those first nine exchanges.

Perhaps my point will be better understood if we consider how the lines *could* have been formulated. Instead of:

You took the children to Lottie's?

The first line of dialogue could have been:

Harry, did you do as I told you, did you take the children to Lottie's?

Eighteen syllables instead of eight. Instead of Harry replying with only three syllables:

I took them, he could have replied with eleven:

Of course I took them, what do you take me for?

Instead of Sarah asking:

They didn't mind? She could have asked:

Were they busy, were they angry, did they mind?

Eleven syllables instead of four. And instead of Harry replying:

No, they didn't mind. He could have replied:

Did you expect Lottie and Hymie to mind? And so on. I think you can see how selection was in operation.

But I can't arrive at any theory or formula which will either ensure I'll get it right every time, for ever, nor can I formulate a process which can be handed on to someone who wants to learn how to write plays. I can tell a young writer he or she must select, and select economically, but I can't teach them *how* to select. I can look at a line they've written and perhaps explain why for me it lacks power, but even then it's only for me, it's a subjective response – an informed and experienced subjective response, perhaps, but a subjective one nevertheless.

And believe me it's all much more complicated than I've been able to explain. For example, those sensibilities, which were at work in 1964 when I wrote a lyrical play about love called *The Four Seasons*, were no longer at work in 1978; so I cut and re-shaped the play, I relaxed the dialogue. In 1964 I needed to write a more intense kind of dialogue than I wrote for *Chicken Soup With Barley* in 1957. And twelve years after writing that intense dialogue I felt a need to relax it again.

Next, briefly, to take up my second argument: dialogue, like form, is dictated by the material. I can't claim to know how other playwrights work, but for me it begins with my material, and by 'material' I mean very specifically not an idea but experience. That is the kind of writer I am – I may have imagination but I don't possess great powers of invention. I don't begin with an idea for a play and then invent characters and plot and situation. I mostly begin with experience, an experience of reality which has made an impression on me. And the only way I can reassemble that experience is through theatre – occasionally through stories, poetry,

TV, film, but mainly theatre. And that experience, that material, *seems always to have told me the shape it wants to be.*

The Kitchen could not have begun anywhere else than in the early morning with the lighting of the ovens and ended with the evening meal. There *were* possible alternatives. I could have alternated between kitchen and restaurant; I could have descended into the homes and private lives of some of the characters. I didn't even consider such alternatives. The wish to write a play about my experiences in a kitchen came to me already dressed in its form – a form that I had experienced in Le Rallye, the kitchen in Paris where I worked for eight months.

Similarly, *Chicken Soup With Barley* came to me in its own form – stretching from the famous anti-fascist demonstrations in the East End of London 1936, a period of innocence and idealism, to the anti-communist uprising in Hungary to 1956, a period of disillusion. And the wish to recreate a love affair came in the form of *The Four Seasons* – winter of unhappiness, spring of slow awakening, summer of love blossoming, autumn of love falling apart. I didn't think, 'wouldn't it be interesting to encase a love affair within the framework of four seasons?' The experience fell into its own shape, and when it did so, when it was ready I wanted to write it.

I could go on about most of the plays in the same way. The form may not have come immediately nor the texture of the dialogue, but when the form did come, when the material revealed its needs, then the sound and rhythm of the dialogue followed. The novelist, Doris Lessing, wrote a story about a diamond merchant who wants to cut the stone for the ring of his wife-to-be. He places the raw diamond on a table and walks round and round it for three days looking at it, contemplating it, trying to understand, to perceive the shape of the diamond contained within the stone. His skill is selecting the right raw material, and then he doesn't *impose* his wishes on that raw material, he gazes and gazes in order to allow the material to reveal its own shape.

Similarly, if I have any talent, it rests in part in selecting material that is more than itself, in selecting material from a full and confusing life that is right for drama rather than merely the stuff of anecdote – small story-telling belonging more to the dinner-table than to the stage. Let me illustrate what I mean by that. It's an illustration I've offered once before in an essay at the beginning of this volume - forgive the repetition. I had a spinster aunt. She had to look after her mother, who died, then a sister, who died. She was hurt by the experience but seemed content to live alone and busy herself with visits to the family. There is nothing remarkable in such an experience. Sitting round a dinner table most guests could probably relate such a family story.

My aunt's history of lonely spinsterhood begins to resonate, begins to become *more than itself,* when I tell you that she used to make crocheted bed-coverings for members of the family and, one day, having made hundreds of squares for a grand-nephew and sewn up all of them except thirty, she stopped. The last thirty remained unattached. She also stopped watering her plants, taking buses to visit us, and washing herself. At one moment on a certain day her spirit wound down to a halt. And because in all of us there is a spirit waiting to give up she entered, on that day, into material for drama, material that was more than it*self* because it could be applied to *all* of ourselves.

So, after choosing the right material there follows the experience of those other skills I referred to: the skills of structure, characterisation, plot, setting, movement, and the skill to be able to select and reassemble dialogue which belongs to the material.

I'd like to end with two lines of dialogue that touch me and might perhaps indicate even more vividly the way I think about dialogue.

The first comes from that old aunt whose story haunts me. Even after she gave up there were still occasions when it was possible to get her moving into spirited conversation, and one day I asked her, did she believe in an after life? Her reply was:

"No I don't! When you're dead you're bloody dead! And that's that!"

Not *when you're dead you're dead* but *when you're dead you're <u>bloody</u> dead*. And to begin she said: *"No I don't"* three syllables, ending with *"and that's that!"* – another three syllables.

"No I don't! When you're dead you're bloody dead! And that's that!"

The second line was uttered in a radio programme about children with terminal illness. One young girl was asked whether she was afraid of dying, to which she replied: *"No, I'm not afraid of dying, I just don't want to be there when it happens."*

If you can analyse that line and understand wherein lies its power you'll begin to understand the nature of theatre dialogue.

Originally written for International Association of Theatre Critics in Rome 1985. Re-written 1993, 1995, and 2002.

11. *What Are We Writers Worth?*

BECAUSE IMPOSSIBLE TO measure, writers measure their worth neurotically. What advance can they command for a book or a play? In which size room are they placed when invited to literary festivals? Who says, when considering upon which playwright to bestow a knighthood, 'him but not him', and why? And which writer dares confess gloom not to be hanging in the National Portrait Gallery? I hung there. Once. By the skin of my teeth. A forlorn Christ-like portrait by the late Joseph Herman with text alongside both out of date and inappropriate. But no longer. Oh to have been the fly on the wall listening to my unworthiness sadly sighed over. Had every play been read and evaluated by a committee or did they dog-like sniff the air in the marketplace? Ah, the marketplace. What mysterious winds blow there, what moon-crazed currents ebb and flow. Is 'sniffing' what happens when our archives are bid for, come up for sale? Noses raised! Nostrils tense! Sniff, sniff! What's he/she worth? Where drift the odours of the day strongest? Sniff, sniff!

The selling of archives is the writer's final reckoning – in this life at least. You sell archives when you need money and space, and the moment you offer is the moment you ask the world to judge you, tell you what it thinks you're worth. Difficult to know how to conduct yourself, what tone of voice to adopt. Should you pretend you hate doing this but oh dear there's no space left in the study? Should you lie? 'I don't really need to sell but, well, academe may just find them moderately of some passing interest.' Or should you boldly confess with what you imagine is disarming honesty that you're simply broke and need to pay a huge income tax bill? Not easy.

I'm a hoarder. I cling to things for their association with periods in my life. We lived in a house in Highgate for twenty-five years, a house where the children grew up amid countless gatherings of family, friends and visitors from abroad, and I've never recovered from having to sell it. I can't let go. Or rather I can but there's pain, and it takes years to recover.

Imagine, then, what it was like contemplating (to say nothing of packing) fifty-six years of a writer's life. We forget how we wrote what we wrote, only the original manuscripts with their crossings-out, their squiggly lines taking passages from one end of the page to the next, can tell us, books full of notes and snatches of possible dialogue, some rather good and never used; dates of when ideas first dawned; lists of reference books revealing what we owed to whom. I had loved reaching back to marvel at how I'd endeavoured. They had gathered over the years in boxes named, numbered and stored in the attic. And they were leaving me. It took three months to box them, and they weighed three and a half tons. It wasn't the packing took the time it was my mania for making lists of contents in minute detail – 130 pages! Well of course! They were travelling thousands of miles away, my children. It was an appalling prospect no matter how thrilling the other prospect of debts wiped out. Like any good parent I needed their names recorded.

Why do we feel this need to hang on to scraps of paper? Not everyone by far. There exist throwers-out as well as holders-on. We hold on for the knowledge that a life happened, effort was expended, something achieved, but off they went: the original manuscripts of thirty-six plays, four collections of stories, non-fiction, poetry, journalism, four books of dreams and probably sixty novels-worth of hand-written diary (the last eleven years are on disk) together with the minutes and reports of organisations plus nearly nine hundred issues of Time Out going back to the first one in August '68 – and much more.

Serious thoughts about selling the archives began when the British Library approached me saying they had spare cash, and were interested. Wonderful! My country loves and respects me after all, I thought. And my beloved manuscripts would be round the corner. The British Library sent an 'expert' to evaluate. The plays were to hand in a metal filing cabinet but to appreciate the full extent of the archives he had to climb a ladder and peer left and right along the attic. I also provided him with a rough list of what was there.

I had calculated a figure for long-term peace of mind rather than one I thought represented either their real worth or their market value: £150,000. The amount 'the expert' advised the British Library to offer was £60,000. How on earth was it arrived at? The figure couldn't possibly represent the years spanned and the effort taken. Nor could it represent the plays' international reputation. It certainly didn't result from the 'expert' reading everything to make judgements of artistic worth. £60,000 hardly represented even sheer bulk!

There could be only one answer: he had sniffed in the marketplace. Plays had been written regularly interspersed with publications of books of fiction and non-fiction but the air was not rich with the playwright's smell. True, there lingered sweet odours from the past and there hovered also a thin but persistent *current* scent of sorts, but that full blast aroma of freshly ground coffee or bacon frying or bread fresh baked was not around. Wesker was not, as the jazz musicians say, cooking that day.

And here we identify the central tension: the purchasing of a living author's archives involves a conflict of perceptions – the perception of the market and the perception of the writer. The writer's perceptions are rooted in aesthetic values; the market's perceptions are amoral. The process of evaluating good and bad art is not a process known to the market, which can rely on nothing but its nose.

January 1999 enter Dr. Thomas F. Staley, Director of The Harry Ransom Humanities Research Centre in The University of Texas at Austin – one of the most sensitive, erudite, sympathetic noses in the archive trade. The diligent doctor flew in on 17 March and climbed the stairs to the attic. I think he was impressed but his manner was more respectful than overwhelmed. "What figure did you have in mind?" he asked. I paused for the merest second and uttered a round figure as near as I could work out in dollars to £150,000 (plus a little bargaining room – high-powered financial negotiator that I was). "$250,000" I said as though there could be no question.

To his credit Dr Staley didn't blanche but could see he was dealing with no slouch here. Here was a giant of high finance who, delicate poet though he be, knew his way around the marketplace. "That's more than we paid for John Osborne's or Tom Stoppard's papers," he said. I suppressed the smile of disdain that was rising to my cheeks and replied: "Oh, but they were not diarists." Whether that was true or not I had no idea but when at sea one must do one's best to walk on water. He would, he said, have to discuss it with his board. Of course!

The months passed. We sold our London house and suddenly the financial pressure was off. An offer came through from Austin in May. $160,000 (£100,000) over three years. What talks between whom had resulted in that figure I wondered? A handsome amount but $90,000 short of my price. I returned with a counter-price of $200,000 and a different division of the payment. Further discussion was needed, and Tom – it was Tom and Arnold by now – said he was coming again to the UK and could we meet? At my suggestion he gallantly made the trek to my workplace in the Black Mountains of Wales where the boxes from the London attic had been transported and were laying, getting damp, in an exposed barn. I hoped, wily tycoon that I was, that not only would he obtain a full view of the archives sprawled around the barn under plastic sheets but he'd be mortified by their plight, and do anything to rescue them – like accept the price I was asking.

Come early September I made lunch for Tom, showed him the spoils in the barn spoiling, and waited.

Come late September a letter arrived saying the board could go no higher than their original offer.

I went back to contacts in the UK who advised me to forget this country, there wasn't either the money or the interest, Texas had superb facilities – let them have it. Which I did. Collapse of tough negotiator. But I had money to repair rotting floors and window frames in the Black Mountain retreat, and lay down sensible drainage. Not enough to rebuild my leaking study but enough to update my computer, lay aside money for grandchildren, and write untroubled for a couple of years.

I don't know what to think about what I've done. Emotions are mixed – relief, regret, loss. I feel secure, bereft, demeaned, flattered. Of course every writer believes their manuscripts are worth more than they receive but there is no way sensibly and with dignity to argue why. What *is* unarguable, however, is the honour bestowed when purchased by a prestigious university. Honour doesn't plug up a leaking roof, and we all would prefer to have been honoured in our own country but – honour is honour.

And we are content.

4th July 2000

12. The Myth of 'a Writer's Theatre'.

MY CONTENTION IS that there is no such institution as 'a writer's theatre'; I speak with the authority of one whose first five plays were performed in The Royal Court – probably the first theatre to lay claim that it was a theatre for writers.

Of course every theatre that mounts a play could be described as a writer's theatre because what is offered, whether by commercial management or state-subsidised management, is written by a writer! But we all know what the description implies: 'A Writer's Theatre' is the boast of an artistic directorship that wishes its policy to be understood as one that gives priority consideration to new writing by new writers. Not, note, a policy simply of new writing but *new writing by new or newish writers*, a policy that could be termed 'ageist'.

The Royal Court, The Bush, The Young Vic and many others lay claim to being 'a writer's theatre'. But is it true? *Can* it be true? What really can it mean? Let's look a little more closely at the boast. We know it doesn't mean that writers read and choose the plays that will fill each season's offerings? It certainly can't mean – to go to the ridiculous extreme – that anyone with a first play can knock at the theatre's door and expect it to be performed; but might it mean that a playwright with a track record could expect his or her next play to be performed? Apart from Sir Alan Ayckbourn being the Artistic Director of The Library Theatre in Scarborough (retired in 2009) where he tried out his plays, I know of few others where a writer has such power of entry.

Let me write a little about the one theatre with which I 'grew up', The Royal Court. There is no doubt that George Devine and Tony Richardson (the late joint artistic directors) cherished and indulged their writers but it didn't stop them initially turning down, one after the other, those first five plays of mine: *Chicken Soup with Barley*, *Roots* and *I'm Talking About Jerusalem* (all launched from The Belgrade Theatre, Coventry, and titled by *The Court as The Wesker Trilogy*; *The Kitchen* – cautiously permitted as a Sunday Night 'production without decor' at the Court; and *Chips With Everything* accepted only after a commercial manager, Bob Swash, offered to co-produce it with the Court. Nevertheless it is the nearest I can get to imagining 'a writer's theatre'. In an essay I wrote for a book celebrating The Royal Court's 25th Anniversary I acknowledged my debt to this glorious establishment, but what really made us imagine it was a genuine 'writer's theatre'?

First, they gave writers a physical base. To be able to walk into that building in Sloane Square at will, pop in to watch rehearsals, meet other theatre people, and feel it was ours gave us an invaluable sense of belonging.

Next, they spotlighted our plays for the world to see. The interest in new drama which The Royal Court engendered and which was given its initial thrust by John Osborne's *Look Back in Anger*, brought the Court to the attention of agents, impresarios and directors from all over the world. We were made 'international writers' overnight. This was a launching from which, fifty years later, personally speaking, I'm still reaping some benefits.

Third, there were the famous writers' gatherings, which took place mainly in a huge room of a house on Chiswick Mall belonging to Anne Piper, one of the group. We talked, played theatre games, tried out our ideas – not all of them productive but always with an air of gaiety and anticipation.

And last, most important of all for me, the Court gave me a team: the late John Dexter, director, and the late Jocelyn Herbert, designer. We made my first five plays together. I can't pretend there was no friction but there is no doubt in my mind that I learned from John how to direct plays, and from Jocelyn the central importance of design, how the wrong set can utterly destroy the careful rhythms a writer weaves into his work. Jocelyn was an inspired designer and a modest human being upon whom Dexter and I leaned for advice in uncertain times, and reassurance in dark and doubting times.

These four elements – the base, the international spotlight, the writers' group and, most important, the team – all culminated in the fifth element: self-confidence. Of course, many things have since conspired to destroy that self-confidence – careless critics, treacherous actors, unadventurous directors; but nothing, I suppose, can really shake that foundation which I received in those first four years of my association with The Royal Court. They didn't like or understand what I wrote, but they took the risk. I'd like to think they trusted the writer but with experience and hindsight I now understand it was the directors – Anderson and Dexter – whom they trusted. But whoever and however, they gave this writer self-confidence and he owes them a debt.

But the question persists: was it 'a writer's theatre'? Despite the enthusiastic reception of *Roots* and *The Kitchen* I still could not expect my next plays automatically to be accepted. The directors, Devine and Richardson, who considered *The Kitchen*, with its 31 actors on stage simulating work in a restaurant kitchen, impossible to stage nevertheless decided that Dexter had earned the opportunity to stage the play. John was confident he knew how to pull such a mammoth work together. He suggested re-writes and a new section – 'The Interlude' – a period of quiet between serving lunch in Act One and serving dinner in Act Two without which the play would not have been as strong. He rehearsed for two weeks on a budget of £100 and the result was electrifying. But Devine and Richardson still didn't bring it in to the following season until another play dropped out and Dexter was called upon to rush a production together which was again a huge success. It has subsequently become the most performed of my plays around the world.

The successful reception of *Chicken Soup with Barley* led to the production of *Roots* which led to the production of *The Kitchen*. But those successes were no guarantee that the Court's management would accept my next play, *Chips With Everything*; they didn't until a commercial management entered the scene. It ran for a year in the West End but was still no guarantee of subsequent productions of my later plays not even under the heading 'New Writing'. So on what basis could The Royal Court claim to be a writer's theatre when they kept rejecting the work of one of their most acclaimed writers? The answer is simple – there exists no such basis. Artistic directors everywhere who claim they are running 'a writer's theatre' are in a state of denial. No such theatre exists nor *can* exist. All plays must be filtered through those directors and, more likely, literary managers with first class degrees in Eng. Lit. and little ability to lift a play off a page, or whose antenna are tilted to detect what is politically correct or (ephemerally) of the moment.

To my detriment I don't write like that. I find myself drawn to universal material and unpopular perceptions, qualities a bold management should cherish; they seem not to, and so I have no home, no base, no team with whom to work on that material, and my file of curious, stuttering, contradictory letters of rejection grows. Artistic Directors admire my plays for their 'powerful' themes, 'passionate dialogue', and 'brilliant' something or other but, but, but ... they do not fit into their artistic policy.

I don't understand the notion of 'artistic policy'. Why is not the artistic policy of every theatre simply to mount a good play regardless of race, colour, gender or age? I call upon Artistic Directors to be honest, move out of their state of denial and confess: that what audiences are permitted to see is not what writers write but what directors want to direct. Admit it, there is no such thing as a writer's theatre, there can only ever be a director's theatre.

On this my 50th anniversary as a playwright I have about half a dozen works, including a musical of *The Kitchen*, looking for a home in this country. Others, like *Denial, The Wedding Feast* and *Shylock* have been performed only in the regions. Fifteen of them have had their world premiers abroad, and a couple of them have never been performed at all.

I don't think I'm the only such writer. There being no writers' theatre many of us feel like Shostakovitch waiting for Stalin to die. We name no names.

Perhaps it's the rudeness that is demoralising. I never send unsolicited scripts to a theatre but write first to ask if they're interested to read a new play. I did so with the West Yorkshire Playhouse. The play was *Denial*, about 'the false memory syndrome' – a hot potato of a play about false accusations of child abuse. They asked to read it. I sent a copy by email. Months passed, I prompted them. They replied that they'd lost the script due to a technical breakdown and would I send another. Which I did. Despite prompts the years have passed in silence. I'm still waiting – even if only for a courteous rejection.

23 March 2009